‘owling At The Top Of The Mountain
“A romping tale of dog training”

Foreword.

Carrie and I became friends by way of the dogs in our lives. We both had adorable Black Labradors, and who doesn't love a Black Lab, right? The diarrhoea, the chewing, and the over-abundance of energy was something that made us gravitate towards each other. Of course, the internet made it so easy to talk and visit, just as if we knew each other and could swing by and visit over tea. My Zamboni girl was destined to leave me for her real owner, a young man who has type 1 diabetes and plays ice hockey anytime he can, but that is what I accept as a service dog trainer. What remained for me after she went home, was the ability to read about Othello and his cool guy adventures. Carrie has taken her feelings and made them gospel in the best way possible, the voice of a dog. I would look forward to her random posts and laugh out loud at the adventures Othello narrated with such skill and "dogs-eye" opinions.

Enter Oberon; the true meaning of the words stretch and grow! Carrie had no idea what she was facing when she got Little Dude, or LD. I could feel the love she had for him in the words she wrote and I cried, not just tears but ugly mouth-open crying, with her when she was advised to think about euthanasia for the puppy. We have an ocean between us and I was beside myself to hold space for her and Oberon. She did the right thing and found the loving grace in herself and Dr.Tom Mitchell (Behavet) to give her a way to work with LD.

I still train service dogs and their handlers, but look forward to the adventures of Othello and LD who will be in my heart because of Carrie. Her game playing, fun loving and laugh-out-loud stories will make you laugh at us humans who think we are in control of what and why a dog does anything we say.

As with all the partners that go to their service homes, I am hoping that I can be crazy Aunt Barb to Othello and Oberon and always a loving space for Carrie, my friend across the pond who has a heart that can hold all the dogs that need her.

Barbara Phillips,
Keystone Handler Academy, Elko, Nevada, USA
www.k9altability.com
@keystonehandler academy

My Gratitude

When I was looking for something extra to go on the back cover of my book, just by chance I received some lovely feedback from a friend in the dog training community. I was so honoured by her words that I asked if I could use them on the back cover.
Being the lovely lady that she is she agreed immediately. I then tentatively decided to ask if anyone else would like to contribute. I was so overwhelmed by the wonderful comments I received that I wanted to show my gratitude and include the following with their kind permission.

I look forward to hearing the latest antics of these two lucky dogs every day. Every day I smile or laugh. Every day I'm impressed. The way Carrie gets inside these boys heads is phenomenal - Jane Hatton

Reading about LD and Othello's antics really sets me up for the day. Carrie's skills of story-telling and dog training are inspiring. This book will be an awesome read – Jo Preston

The ongoing adventures of the 2 O's and how they are training Carrie has been a constant source of entertainment and learning – Noeleen Price

I look forward to reading about the adventures of Othello and LD, you really bring their characters to life and at times make me laugh out loud – Sharon Maddy

Be prepared to seriously startle anyone in close proximity as you laugh, cry, and jump up and down shouting "YES! YESS!!!" This is a tale of two dogs and their human … and how they form, evolve and enjoy their relationship through fun, games, and a lot of mud … and wine … definitely no kibble. You must read this book – Kerry Neal

When I read your quotes, I know that I am not alone with dog training issues, and even feel mine are not really that bad, great to read your tales, they always make me laugh – Jenny Scott

A fabulous account of Carrie's days with the 2 O's. Gorgeous dogs, a few tears, tons of laughter and a generous slurp of wine. What's not to love? – Kirsty Jenkins

We look forward every day to reading Othello and LD's adventures, they always raise a smile and a bonus when our dog Barnaby gets to join the "chat". Dog lovers will adore the world of these two – Jenny Brown

LOL canine adventures of Othello and Oberon (a.k.a. LD) – their antics are guaranteed to make your day – especially when you realise you are not alone with your creative and mischievous furry companions – Suzanne Lea

Early in my discovery of posts from Carrie, I HAD to ask "Will you write a book with these?" Imagine my delight when the response came back that she would! Oberon and Othello are master storytellers – Robin Lambert

I happened upon the adventures of the 2 O's quite by accident and have had chuckles and outright belly laughs as I have read the antics of Othello and Oberon. Thanks for bringing your adventure to the outside world – Martha Gerow

Carrie, your posts and updates on the adventures and misadventures 😉 of Othello and LD have brightened our days, given us hope, soothed us in trying times and given us a lot of joy and laughter. Thank you – Susie Gutierrez

Anecdotes from The Top Of The Mountain bring sunshine and laughter into every day – Catherine Haywood

Hop aboard the daily Merry-Go-Round of dog ownership and training with Othello, Oberon and Carrie – Joy Green

Reading your adventures and many ups and downs and how you deal with them with humour and honesty, has made me laugh out loud and sob even louder. While going through the same things with a similar little dog it has been difficult to keep going at times, and I found your posts exactly when I needed to. It's kept me pushing harder seeing the progress you and your pack have made. Thank you so much for sharing – Sarah Miller

Just love your honesty and humour and we need that in abundance!! Your style of writing will appeal to just about everyone, you don't need to be a dog owner to love your stories. Can't wait to see you in print Carrie, you are too funny! – Linzi Benham

When I am having a bad day, there is always the two O's to look up to for a good laugh or a warm moment. Thank you so much Carrie, for sharing their thoughts with us. They are priceless – Josiane Ménard Cuerrier

Reading you training adventures (and misadventures) always brightens my day and makes the world a better place – Julie Thompson

I always look forward to reading your posts – can't wait to read the book – Sarah Patreane

Following your adventures, the honesty of the relationship and all the love that all of you put into every step is truly inspirational , thank you !!! – Lola Ocampo Miño

You have made me smile every day with your adventures. You are an inspiration to us all – Jo Grin-Yates

So happy you decided to help Othello and Oberon write their book (let's face it, they are the authors!). – Jillian Aspinall

Can't wait for this to come out Carrie, will definitely be getting a copy, love reading your posts of the two O's xx - Karen Lucas

Sharing the tears, laughter, fears and progress of Othello and Oberon has been a regular "must read" for me. Carrie's dedication to relaying the dogs' antics and finding humour in every puddle make her an angel - Hazel Markou

In Memory of Kate Boothby,
25/4/64 – 23/10/19
The very best of the best.

Acknowledgements.

The list of people I want to thank is long, and my gratitude is deep.
My daughter Jo, who helped me in countless ways and stopped me from giving up on this book! Also, for helping with the cover design and illustrating the seasons inside these pages.
My sons Ffinbar and Poric for just being themselves.
My husband Richard, for being a good father and husband.
Barbara Phillips, who was one of the first people to encourage me to write a book.
Joyce Morel, who reached out to support me when Oberon was at his most challenging and prompted me to become a dog trainer.
Karen Scott, for the laughs we share on our journey with our dogs.
Jud Gretton, for offering to proofread this book.
Terry, for being a jolly good sport!
Alison Howard for the wonderful illustrations of Othello and Oberon inside this book.
Dr. Tom Mitchell and Lauren Langman, the founders of Absolute Dogs. Their training methods have brought back the fun for me and my dogs. Each of their games referred to in this book uses concept training to help reshape a dog's brain while building a wonderful bond.
My friends, dogs, and other animals who have made this book possible.

Introduction

Welcome to the shared journey between me and my wonderful dogs. You can follow us as we navigate our way through sometimes pulse-racing anxiety, often belly-wobbling laughter and, thankfully, a dose of calmness. I would love you to share the laughs and the tears, the highs and the lows, as we embrace the path to a better life together.

I have been lucky enough to have dogs as part of my life from a young child, and then have my own dogs as an adult. I had trained them with reasonable success and felt they were pretty-well-adjusted and happy dogs. Othello, my beautiful Labrador, is the keeper of a huge part of my heart. He struggled with how to calmly interact with other dogs and was anxious of anything novel, so when I was looking for a new way to train him I came across Absolute Dogs, and a really amazing fun way to train. A style of training based around games and rewards, it put the fun back into my relationship with my dogs. Using Concept training, it helped to reshape the brains of my dogs, while building an amazing relationship.

Oberon, my adorable but somewhat anxious Cockapoo, came into my life at 11 weeks old rather unexpectedly, and has been without a doubt the dog that nearly broke me! Between them, Othello and Oberon have taught me so much about myself and about dogs. They were the inspiration for me to go on and qualify as a dog trainer. I also decided to learn much more about the way their brains work. They are the fuel for this book, which started as an occasional post into an online dog training group. With encouragement from the members, it became a daily event. The members planted the seed for this book - and it's fair to say, some of them even demanded it! The Games mentioned (apart from Knicker Elastic) are to be credited to Absolute Dogs.

The rest of the crew at home start with Truffles, a Border collie, who generally has the sweetest nature but has no real interest in other dogs and would prefer they remained off her radar. I also have Piper, a Norwich terrier and Tofu, a Jug. Tofu is always guaranteed to lift your mood and Piper is a "goodie-two-shoes" and very much a mummy's boy. They are, almost completely, silent accomplices in this tale but still very important family members. Other furry and feathery friends are a house rabbit called Timothy and some rescue ducks. Human family members include my husband Richard, my daughter Jo and my sons Ffinbar and Poric. Since we added

more play into our lives, we have become a much happier (and mostly well behaved) family of humans and dogs!

This book is a year in the life of Othello and Oberon, as they share their thoughts on what they think of my training skills. They vocalise their humorous opinions on the day-to-day challenges of living with humans. Oberon has a very unique way of speaking and I'm sure you will adapt to it very quickly. After all, he is just a baby. 😊 However, if you struggle at all, then there is a dictionary at the end. 😊

With reference to Absolute Dogs games. They are so versatile that they often fit into more than one of the concepts that we want to grow in our dogs. However, to make your read easier, here's a very brief explanation. There are many more concepts than the ones I've used here.
Boundary games: Teaching a dog to stay at/on our chosen location.
DMT (Distraction Mark Treat): To help our dogs Disengage from distractions.
Middle: To teach a dog the value of staying in close Proximity to us.
Kapow: Teaching Proximity and Disengagement
Leg Weaves: A Proximity game.
Two Paws On: To build Confidence and Optimism.
Toy Switch: Helps to teach Disengagement.
Cone Game: Teaching Confidence and Optimism.
Mouse: Helping to build stillness and Self-Control in our dog.
Crazy Lady: Disengagement.
For more information about Absolute Dogs contact them at absolute-dogs.com

This is by no means a novel, more a book that you may simply pick up, flip to a random page, and read when the mood strikes. All I hope is that it adds some joy and a few laughs to your day when you do.

If you would like to contact me as a dog trainer or to reflect on this book then here are my details:

Carrie Crompton, Powys, Wales.
Email:totmdogtraining@gmail.com
Website:https://www.topofthemountaindogtraining.co.uk

Autumn
23nd Sept – 20st Dec
2019

‘owling At The Top Of The Mountain
“A romping tale of dog training”

Chapter One
‘Minibus or monster?’

19th September 2019

Let me introduce myself.

I am a 4-year-old black Labrador and Carrie named me Othello.

Carrie thinks she has been training ME but if I am honest, I think most of the issue is at her end of the lead.
I will admit that historically I have been a bit of a puller and the occasional barker but I am a dog and that’s how we dogs behave, unless someone shows us a different way.

Life is pretty exciting since Carrie found a new way of training, and we’ve been having great fun with games.

Anyway, back to today …

To be totally honest I worry about Carrie!!

Take this morning for instance. We're stood outside the gate and it's very foggy, and from nowhere came what looked like a massive monster with red eyes making some sort of beeping noise!

Well, I was a cool as a cucumber (I really have to be or Carrie seriously over-reacts, pulling on the lead and being loud. I AM training it out of her though).
Anyway, she appeared to feed the Oldest Boy to the monster!!! ... its side opened up, and he may well have been eaten alive; I could see his hand at the window as it went off down the road growling!!!!
I was thinking of making a fuss about it but then I thought about the extra food that would be available.

We didn't see any of the usual people we see on walks today and although I don't like to be unkind, I'm pretty certain they are avoiding us.
Carrie gets all silly when she sees them, waving and calling out, I'm trying really hard to just pretend I haven't seen them so she gets out of the habit.
She says it's about getting me used to novelty, but I think she may be a little unhinged 😉

I mistook some cows in a field for huge black dragons with smoke coming out of their noses, and what appeared to be a baby dragon with them.
I could just make them out through the fog, huffing and puffing. Any second I was expecting flames to start licking out of their mouths and to hear the flapping of wings.
Luckily, as I got closer, I realised what they were and breathed a deep sigh of relief. Heaven knows how Carrie would have acted if they HAD taken flight.
I realised that we had seen them last week, and Carrie had been cooing over the little Dragon and pointing at it. She obviously thinks it's very cute; let's face it, she's a sucker for attractive black animals 😉
I'm cool with it though, as she keeps telling me how Niiiiice they are and giving me a treat. This Niiiiice word has been used an awful lot since we started this new training.
One thing that's for certain though, is that a treat follows it, so she can Niiiiice as much as she wants!

I'm very thankful that she's grown out of the fox poo phase though. Not that long ago I was having to roll in it because, oddly, she seemed to love me doing it.
She'd get soooo excited and be jumping up and down with what I can only assume was pleasure and squealing too.
After more usage of the Niiiice word, I've finally got her to the stage where I can just glance at it and we can move on.

Why she has to keep telling me how nice it is I just don't know (frankly I think it's disgusting stuff) but the bonus is she gives me a treat which is a vast improvement on her previous behaviour.

Now, another strange thing is that she cannot make her mind up which way we're going. One minute we're walking in a particular direction and then we're going back the other way.
She can't walk in a straight line for toffee; she keeps doing funny little circle shapes.
I heard her telling someone that it's called Figure Of Eight Walking and it's to help build calmness.
Obviously, she's practising with me before she tries it on those terrible terriers, Tofu and Piper …

I wonder if any of this behaviour is anything to do with what happened the other day?

She was being odd again, lying on the floor and then sitting up over and over with a weight in her hands. I thought perhaps she was having some sort of episode, so I decided the best thing to do was to walk behind her as she started to lie down again. I knew it would support her back and let her rest.
Well, what a lot of noise she made!
How was I supposed to know that if I stopped her lying down the weight would smack her in the face????
I've heard that concussion can lead to strange behaviour, which might explain an awful lot!!

Anyway … back to the walk.

I thought after we'd done some of the erratic circle walking we might make it home without event, but once again I had to be patient with her. She stood talking to a funny-smelling person for ages about haylage. I was trying to catch her eye an awful lot to say "let's get moving" but she was pretty much ignoring me. So, in the end, I sat patiently looking up at her for at least 10 minutes. On the plus side she seemed to get fixated on feeding me treats and I wasn't doing anything at all, just sitting there. It seems that if I sit quietly, food just falls out of her hand without her even thinking about it.

See what I have to put up with???

I think head injuries can take some time to fix though.

I completely intend to go to sleep on my bed now and ignore her because she exhausts me. Hopefully she'll manage to open the door to the postman today without me having to get up and talk to him 😉

Why I got landed with such an odd one defeats me!

Lots of love from,
Your friend Othello xxx

20th September 2019

Carrie really got her knickers in a bunch yesterday afternoon.

We were out walking, and I was minding my own business really.
We walked past a house where there is often a dog calling to me behind the gate and I just ignore it. To be honest I still don't understand why Carrie keeps telling me it's Niiiice, but I get a treat so I'll suck it up.
That dog uses a lot of energy for nothing, so I've concluded that, like Carrie, it's had a blow to the head at some point!
Anyway, when we walked past it had a sidekick with it and boy could they shout.
Well, there are limits, so I did a bit of cussing back and jumping towards it.

If I'm totally honest, it didn't quite work the way I planned as Carrie hadn't clipped my lead on properly and when I jumped the lead came free, so I ended up across the other side of the road and got a bit of a shock!!
I blustered it out a bit and shouted to the dogs about language in front of a lady, and then I went back to Carrie.
I try really hard not to bark at other dogs but two of them together was just too much for me.

We went home and then a bit later walked past that house again.
Well, if she thought I was going to pull out all the stops again she was wrong, I had very much made my point and the sidekick dog didn't say a word.
"Old Faithful" did a bit of chatting, so I just rolled my eyes and walked on.
Fortunately, Carrie remembered her training and although she kept up the irritating Niiiice, she did give me loads of especially tasty treats.

Today was such a contrast.

When we went for a walk this morning we almost fell over some bloke when he came around a corner.
I've seen him before, but I didn't recognise him at first because his head looked a different shape without a cap and he was carrying a rucksack.
I know how Carrie can get stressed by changes, so I took it all in my stride and she remained calm.
She did some of her default behaviour, which is feeding me, but I'm prepared to overlook that as any small improvement is worth rewarding.

We are making progress with calmness, which is a godsend really, because a very excitable woman came up the road and excitement always sends Carrie's energy levels sky high.
I can see her point though, the woman seemed to have no social graces, no butt sniffing, no play-bowing, just straight into grabbing Carrie and hugging her.
Thank heaven I've put the work in with Carrie or she might have bitten her today 😂

With love to you all,
Othello xxx

21st September 2019

Frankly, this is going to be a short post because I'm exhausted after Carrie's shenanigans this morning.

Mostly I walk her myself as the brunt of her training is in my paws.

I let the other dogs take her later because there are three of them to share the load, and she is normally behaving better after I've walked her.

However, I decided to take Piper with me this morning and if I'm honest it was a mistake.
He just hangs around by her feet gazing up at her all the time. If that's what the other two do as well, it's no wonder my job is so hard!!
Anyway, every time I took my eyes off her this morning she dashed off!!
The first couple of times I thought she was just excited about the new surroundings as we were deep in the forest, so I didn't stress too much.
The next time I looked away she was hiding behind a tree (I assumed she was relieving herself, as we dogs do, but she was just loitering). When I caught up with her she ran off again with one of my flipping toys!!
I got her walking calmly again on the track and I did a few sits and let her revert to her comfort behaviour of feeding me a few treats, when blow me she suddenly started squealing like a stuck pig and ran off again.
She was leaping around like a woman possessed. It's all very embarrassing for me but Piper just carries on googly-eyeing her.
On one occasion she ran off, but because she called out my name I was able to catch her quickly which was lucky because she'd dropped even more of my breakfast!
I've decided that I need to keep a very close eye on what she's doing with my food!

There were a couple of men on two-wheeled growling and roaring machines in the forest.
I really felt that I should run and tell them to stay away from her as she's so unpredictable, but I decided it might be safer if I got her to keep eye contact with me.
She obviously saw them but stayed close anyway, which in my mind was a win.

I'm about to go and have a rest as she has settled on her boundary. Boundary is the new word she uses for our beds, so the sofa must be her boundary as that's where she sits 😊 I don't suppose she'll stop there for long but I'm just going to pretend to be asleep and hope someone else watches her.

Yours,
Othello xxx

22nd September 2019

I'm very happy to say that the sidekick wasn't at the gate this morning. "Old faithful" called out to me but Carrie behaved beautifully and I allowed her to feed me treats to encourage that behaviour.

She is a mystery to me though, with her erratic conduct.

There was a spider in our bedroom and it did a very polite "meet and greet" by walking on her shoulder.
Now, you would have thought someone had attacked her!!! She screamed and started leaping around like she'd eaten a chilli. I just ignored her as I don't understand what the fuss is about!
As I am a good sharer, I was cool with having an extra guest in our bed.

However, just to confirm how weird she is, when we were out on our walk and there was some poor bloke who seemed to be being eaten by the inside of a car, she didn't even react! Just kept saying how Niiice it was.
All I could see was his legs and the rest of him was being devoured so it wasn't niiice for him! I suppose it does show she's getting calmer though. Pretty much every day there is someone disappearing into the inner reaches of that car.
Kind of proves my point about how difficult humans are to train!!

When Carrie says "car" to me I have to jump up into ours, so I'm mighty glad that our one is friendly!

I am also trying to build up her confidence in water but so far I can't get her any closer than the river bank.
I've tried running in with a toy but she won't follow me. I think I might try something with a higher value like her phone next time 😉😉

She had another of those "can't make up her mind" spells this morning. One minute she wanted me on the bench and then she didn't.

We did that several times until she decided she wanted me off the bench. I don't mind too much because I get treats.

Bye for now!
Your long-suffering friend,
Othello xxx

23rd September 2019

Morning from sunny Wales.

I've had to be incredibly helpful again this morning as Carrie had problems with her legs.
She was taking these huge steps and waving a treat under my nose, so I worked out that she wanted me to walk between her legs to stop her from falling over.
To be honest, I'm glad no one saw us because she looked like her feet were made of lead and I was weaving all over the place like I've seen people do at parties.

There were some amazing smells in the forest today but after her running off at the weekend I did not take my eyes off her, so she stayed close and focused.
I'm afraid I did abandon her for a few seconds when this puppy came running towards me down the track.
I explained to him about her issues and he came back to help me with her. He did a lot of trying to stop her falling over front ways by standing up on his back legs and holding her up.
I then sat by her side and watched her very carefully in case she started acting up while she wittered on to the other dog's person ...
They were funny talking about house training and crates as if they were trying to teach us something 😂😂
Sometimes I just cry with laughter at how simple-minded they are! We all know that training them to let us outside to toilet when we are puppies can take ages because they just can't apply themselves to anything properly. Always wandering off and forgetting to keep their eyes on us for those all-important signals. Thank goodness I'm long past needing help.

We saw many pheasants in the woods. It would have been a joy to chase them but who knows where Carrie would run off to if I did?

To compound my confusion, since we started this new training, she has decided to stop putting my food in a bowl.
On the positive side though, she's finally worked out that we dogs like to do something fun for our food and sometimes even search it out 😊
She's taken to throwing some of my breakfast amongst a load of plastic bottles and cardboard boxes.
It's stuff that comes out of her recycling bin and I have to pick my food out from around it and between it.
Can you believe it? I get to rummage around in rubbish with guaranteed snacks and no tutting sounds!

Remember earlier that I mentioned the monster that ate the Oldest Boy? It clearly didn't like the taste of him because it brought him back and spat him out later that day.
I have mixed feelings about that because I was looking forward to his share of the food 😕

Bye for now,
Othello xxx

24th September 2019

Good morning from Othello in a very wet Wales.
I'm so thankful that we play more games now, because I didn't get dragged out in the rain this morning.
Not that long ago Carrie would have thought that we needed to be outside trudging along, whatever the weather, but today we've been training indoors. Which in my opinion is much better than three boring walks a day 😊

She decided that I needed a new bed and the new one is super weird (no surprises there considering who bought it 😂😂)

It doesn't just lie on the floor so I can't ruck it up and drag it around if I want.
This one stands there all tensed up like it's super proud of itself 😳

Personally, I would rather pretend it's not there, and then perhaps it will just go away, but Carrie has been doing something called Boundary Games and I think the idea is that I'm supposed to get on it of my own accord.
I'm slightly confused because she used to just say "bed" in a funny voice before, but now I seem to have a choice about it.
The plus side is that I can just play dumb and if I just look at it I'll get a treat, although I'm not that impressed and I'd rather just eat the bag of treats (which I tried when she wasn't looking 😂😂😂😂😳 shhhh).
In my defence, I had to rummage through garbage and noisy tins to get a morsel this morning, so I was hungry, and the treat bag was just sitting there 😉
I did get on that new bed thing a few times because I can't help myself when it comes to a snack or two 😁 but I don't like how it feels under my delicate little paw paws.
Hopefully, she'll get bored with it and I can go back to humping my other bed, which is a really fun activity and I know she loves me doing it because she gets soooo animated 😂😂

On another subject, I've had to have more strong words with Piper.
He came back from his walk yesterday grinning to himself and thinking he was smelling heavenly.
He is such a people pleaser and so he only went and rolled in fox poo!!
He said he just loves to see Carrie so happy, leaping around and all excited!! I've told him that if he indulges her again then he can forget coming on my sofa!

Gotta go as I've just remembered where one of the treats rolled to!

Love from,
Othello xxx

24th September 2019

It's Othello again. I know I don't normally post twice in one day but I'm busting with excitement!!
I've just found my Super-Power!! Carrie got this thing which dispenses treats and I have totally worked out how awesome I am!!
All I have to do is look at her and a treat comes out of this machine!! I have double telepathy!!! I look at her and think "I want a treat" and my Super-Power bounces off her and makes the machine throw out a treat ... sometimes it even does lots of treats!
I'm so in control now!! I've tried glancing at her sideways, sitting down and looking at her and doing a really quick look away and back ... everything I do works 😂😂😂
I am so going to abuse my power 🙈

Lots of love,
Othello xxx

25th September 2019

Had a walk in the rain this morning and I didn't eat the baby wren that flew in front of my nose, even though it could have made a tasty morsel.
I did get a treat for not doing that, but it was tough call – that wren may have tasted better.
I'll try and get one next time Carrie runs off and give you an update 😉

I had some fun with Carrie today; we did some great training.
We played a game which I love, as all I have to do is run through her legs and I get treats!
Afterwards I ran and jumped into a muddy ditch 😂😂 her face went a really lovely puce colour and I'm certain I saw steam coming out of her ears, but she didn't say a thing!
I waited for her face to go back to its normal colour and then I did it again 😂😂😂

In the old days she would have got way more animated. She didn't seem that happy after I'd done that, so I did lots of grinning up at her and getting her to make eye contact and letting her give me treats 😉

We walked past a field and a load of sheep ran off from the fence.
I just ignored them as they are such stupid creatures.

We saw a woman with some dogs before she saw us and I gave them a little woof as a greeting, you should have seen that woman jump, lol!!
We had to walk past them, and her dogs just stood and pulled towards me as I'm so awesome.
Carrie was super-focused on feeding me treats, something called DMT which I think means Don't Make Trouble.
I always keep a close eye on her to make sure she doesn't make trouble though – I've told you before how over-excited she can get.

I'm hoping to use my Super-Power again later with that cool machine.

Love from,
Othello xxx

27th September 2019

Hi peeps,

Carrie has said that we are going to play games at home today because we need a day off from walking.

It might be something to do with that cat that was whispering obscenities at me yesterday and I scuttled it 😂😂 Boy, you should have seen how big its tail got 😂😂
I was hoping to play that particular game again today but Carrie's being a party pooper about that 😾 She takes life way too seriously sometimes 😕

I thought I might just tell you about something that happened in the summer.

Most often back then, Carrie used to walk me and the other dogs together and we would quite often play frisbee.
I look back on those days fondly as they were wild, impulsive, days and I would get worked up into a real frenzy.
Sadly, I have to play more nicely now as Carrie is all about calm.
Anyway, we were out on our walk, me and the rest of the gang, and Carrie was tossing that frisbee in her normal erratic way.
To be honest, her throwing resembles a baby giraffe trying to breakdance. On this occasion she was at least getting it to soar through the trees some of the time, and me and the others were chasing it and bringing it back. I say some of the time because she often hits trees when she throws it …sigh.
I always get to take it all the way back to her because I just body slam the other dogs out of the way (it's a dog-eat-dog situation).
Zoom! It went off, and Truffles and I pursued it, but we were in for a big surprise as it landed right in a wasp's nest, and those wasps were raging.
The terrible terrier guys were giving it large at the top of the hill but neither of them are much cop at putting the leg work in, so they remained at a safe distance cheering us on.
Truff and I ran out of there like our tails were on fire. Carrie did a lot of random swiping and got us to go in a pond to get rid of those crazy insects.
Poor Truffles was stung quite a few times, but I managed to outwit those pesky stripe jackets.

Round One to me 👍

Well, as you know, lightning does not strike twice in the same place, but it can strike somewhere else!
Two days later in a different part of the forest, the baby giraffe struck again!
This time it was me, her, and the Youngest Boy and we had gone off-piste right into the woods.
When that frisbee struck, we were doomed as we were just a few feet away and trapped by fallen trees.
Those wasps were seething and out to get revenge ... we ran as best as we could with Carrie screaming "save yourselves" and thrashing around as they flew up her sleeves in full attack mode.

She was shedding clothes as she ran and looked like the previous blow-to-the-head behaviour might be making a comeback!
Luckily, those wasps preferred the look of her to us. I escaped with only a couple of stings and Youngest Boy got off unscathed.

Result: A score draw.

Dear reader, you would hope the story would end there, but I'm sorry to say it did not.
A further two days went by, and off she and I trundled on another walk and you've got it, she surpassed herself and once more threw me to the lions! (or wasps in this case).

I was out of those woods like a squirrel up a tree!!

Common sense would suggest that we would leave the scene and not look back ... but you know common sense and Carrie are not good bed mates, and from here on I knew that it would end badly.
She was muttering about not sacrificing another frisbee to those evil wasps!!

I can now confirm that what happens if you poke a stick into a hornet's nest also applies to poking a stick into a wasp's nest!!
Yes, we got that frisbee, but she also performed what I now call the "woodland striptease" yet again while we ran for our lives!!!

Round 3 was definitely a win for the wasps.

I cringe with embarrassment every time I think of her running around in her undercrackers and pray that no one saw her, although I fear that they did, and we will be mocked for many years to come.

Lots of love,
Othello xxx

28th September 2019

Afternoon Friends!

I had a very boring morning as I had to sit in the car for a while when Carrie went into town.
It was OK really because she was jawing to some geezer about tyres, and then I got out to have a sniff around and pee where other dogs had peed.
I never usually go there, so they'll think there's a new kid on the block 😂😂
There were two other blokes standing around yacking, but they weren't even slightly interesting, so even though Carrie was DMTing me I didn't have trouble on my mind.

I did pull a blinder when we got home though because Carrie hadn't noticed the sheep out on the other side of the road, so I scuttled it before she could say a word and I got a bonus mouthful of sheep poo 😂😂😂🎉🎉
I did go straight back when she shouted "ball" and got a good play, so all in all it was a big win for me.
I hope that sheep is there tomorrow 😉

Then some bloke came to look at some work that needed doing in the garden.
I did try a half-hearted jump up at him, but he seemed to know about dogs and stopped me.
Then Carrie got me to sit by her side and gave me treats.
We had a wander around the garden with the bloke and I ignored him as there was just no fun to be had.
Apparently, he's going to make an area where me and the other guys can do something called agility.
Not sure what it is but I hope it involves food 😉

Later, we had a walk and I got Carrie to feed me lots of treats by ignoring things.
I really like playing the new game "Middle" and it always makes Carrie really happy.
Standing between her legs for treats is a pretty easy thing to do 😊
I sometimes sneak a few Middles in without being asked if I'm feeling peckish.

I'm a little bit disappointed because I've been trying to get treats out of that machine by just staring at it, but my Super-Power doesn't seem to work today.
On the plus side I can work it by staring at Carrie and touching a ball on a stick which isn't even slightly arduous.
Going for a kip now but it might be short lived as the rabbit is out and I may fall foul of its jumping games.

Love from,
Othello xxx

30th September 2019

It's Othello here and I'm just itching to tell you about yesterday afternoon.

Carrie took me to see her friend Terry and he is the bestest person in the whole wide world 💕😍💕😍

When we get to the town he lives in, I always start whining with excitement because I know I'm going to have the best fun in the entire Universe 💕💕💕💕😍😍😍😍

We got to his house and Carrie told me to "sit" before she opened the back of the car, which I did, but as soon as there was enough space I was out of that car and at his front door 😂😂

His two dogs were indoors barking like crazy 'cos they loooooove us coming to visit.

Then Terry opened the door, and the fun began!!!

I rushed in, Carrie stepped in, and Murphy body slammed Carrie into the wall 'cos he loves her to bits.
Bella then rushed over.

I pushed past and dashed into the utility room and stuck my head into a bag of dog food and gobbled that food down until I could hardly breath ... OMG ... I love Terry and I love his house!!
Then Murphy body slammed Carrie into the table, and then into the chair!!
We were having an absolute blast.
It was just like dog heaven 💞💞💞💞

When Carrie sat down Murphy jumped up on her knee. She gently helped him down, but he did it over and over and over 😂😂😂😂
His tongue was lolling out with excitement, I was rushing around hoping to get back to that bag of food.

Terry and Carrie were trying to drink tea.

Bella then stole Terry's lunch off the table while he was trying to get Murphy off Carrie.
Then for some reason Bella started growling at me.
It was like a dog playground 😂😂😂😂

They did persuade us to lie down quietly for a while because they wanted to "talk". Murphy kept creeping across the floor so we could play touchy, touchy, wriggly, wriggly, which we both adore!

Then we all piled into Carrie's car and went to the showground.
Terry is the best frisbee thrower in the entire galaxy, but Carrie wouldn't let him throw one as she said I needed to calm down. I just ran along by his side and then in front of him and then at his other side, for nearly the whole hour, with my tongue lolling out.
Bella kept running off into the distance chasing squirrels and rabbits.
Murphy looned around and jumped up at Carrie.
And then Terry threw sticks into the pond and we fetched them and then he sent his dogs to chase squirrels and although I'm not supposed to do that, I ran with them.
Then they hunted for rabbits.

Although she was right by us, I couldn't hear Carrie's voice sometimes 😉
I wasn't going to listen to her 'cos Terry is my bestie 💞💞

I did go to Carrie at the end to have my lead on because she had a ball and I really, really, really, love a ball!

To be totally honest she could have stayed in the car, 'cos I just didn't notice her on the walk 😉

I used to see Terry about two or three times a week with Carrie and we always had the very best fun, but we don't go so often now. I just can't imagine why???????

Can't wait until the next time, just thinking about it makes me breathless 😂

Yours, still excitedly!
Othello xxx

Chapter Two
'Knicker Elastic'

1st October 2019

Morning from Othello.

Everyone knows I love a bit of crazy, but it was real Crazyville out there this morning!!

It was pouring with rain which meant my food was getting super soggy in Carrie's hand.
I was trying to be helpful and gobble it really quickly, but there must have been something wrong with Carrie's hand as she kept clamping it into a fist.
Talk about hard work!
I had to be especially sweet and gentle before I could get it ... sigh.

Then for some reason I had to keep jumping on and off a bench. It made no sense to me, but there was food involved so I was my usual compliant self 😁

Carrie did a lot of pointing at a horse that was in a field with a coat on but it didn't seem very exciting to me, but again I got food.

We walked past the house where "Old Faithhful" lives on the way home, and he called out just as a farmer's noisy machine came around the corner!

I swear I heard Carrie gulp and I was considering giving a pull, but before I could Carrie produced a ball and I was transfixed ... I love a ball soooooo much and I got to carry it 💕💕💕💕💕

Very occasionally I love Carrie very much 😍

As we got to the bus shelter some bloke popped out from its darkness and startled me.
Previously that would have been worth a kick-off, but of course I remained calm and let Carrie give me treats while they nattered on ... yawn.

That was ok though because the magic ball came back out.

See what I mean? Crazyville!!

Love from,
Othello xxx

2nd October 2019

Morning!

It's a stunning morning here all frosty and full of delicious smells.

Had a bit of a shock first thing as we'd just left home and turned the corner when two big dogs appeared snarling and barking.
Well, I just gave them my very best hard bear-stare and immediately looked back at Carrie to see if they had scared her.
She was Ok and gave me some yummy treats to sooth herself.

I'm surprised I'm not suffering this morning with a sore neck as I was playing with the electronic treat dispenser yesterday. I was whipping my head round so fast to look at Carrie and then back to get my treats, that I think I've got whiplash 😂

I quite like the target thing as it looks like a ball. I'm not allowed to play with it which seems a bit unfair, but I cope as I still get treats 😊
I still can't get the cats under control with my Super-Power though, but it does work on the new rubbish bin. If I get close to it, I can make it pop open without touching it 😂😂

We did something called Foot Targeting yesterday afternoon which seemed a bit silly to me, so I just kept walking around the board.
Carrie was being super mean with the treats when I did that, so to humour her I put my feet on it and she became very generous.

I find with Carrie that I have to try several training methods before she understands that I want those treats😕

That's the problem with not having a very bright human!

We're going to have a quiet day apparently as Carrie has stuff to do.

Suits me as it keeps her occupied while I grab some zzzzzz.

Love from,
Othello xxx

3rd October 2019

Hi, it's Othello "the good boy" here.

I know I'm a good boy because Carrie told me about 100 times this morning 

We had such a blast on our walk!

Carrie has invented a game called "The Knicker Elastic Game" and it's such a hoot 😂
What happens is ... I get to run ahead and then without saying anything Carrie

stops walking and she counts in her head how many seconds it takes me to notice.
Then once I've noticed, she counts how many seconds it takes me to run back to her. Sounds like fun, eh?
While I'm running back, she's doing a crazy dance and when I get to her I get a big hug and a tasty treat or two.

I've never really been much of a huggy boy but I really like it now.
Sometimes I even lie across her when we're sitting down together. I used to just lie at the other end of the sofa or the bottom of the bed.

After we played that, a lady came along with some dogs and I did think about jumping up at her but Carrie called me, so I turned on a sixpence and ran back.
She got really smiley then and gave me good treats and got my ball out.
The lady said what a gorgeous boy I was and Carrie said I was "a joy" 😊😊😊
One of her dogs was a bit snappy so I just sat nicely by Carrie's side and ignored the wretch 😂😂

When they had gone, we played some ball for a while and then carried on wandering along until a pheasant just flew up in my face.
Now, let's face it, there was so much fun to be had there! But I just ran back to Carrie and got super tasty treats.
Carrie just kept saying "You're such a good boy ", "I'm so proud of you " and giving me little hugs.
We all knew I was a good boy anyway. Didn't we? 😉

Love from,
Othello xxx

5th October 2019

Very quiet day here as Carrie has been working on the garden, preparing for mine and my buds little agility area, and I wasn't allowed to help 😕
I did try to muck in but I could tell I wasn't really welcome.

I was only intending on going to tidy up the sheep poo that Carrie's sheep had left behind, but apparently I wasn't needed!!
Can't understand why not 😉
The man is coming to start on the area on Thursday if it's not raining (being a pessimist I reckon we'll be waiting until about March next year!)

We've had time to do some training with my favourite piece of kit, and I have to say I'm enjoying it so much 😁
My Super-Power has developed so that I don't even need to look at Carrie!!
I lie there and treats just fall out of the machine 😂😂
I'm not overly impressed when it stops feeding me, because I have to move and touch the ball on the stick. I'm not allowed to play with it either.
I am hoping to train that part out of Carrie though 😂

Carrie is taking me to see Terry tomorrow, so we're bound to have a blast 😂😂

We're going to play some games now. I'd better go.
Bye for now.

Love from,
Othello xxx

8th October 2019

Othello here with a report on this morning's walk!
There were some horses having fun skipping around in a field and they made me jump!!
Luckily, I stopped myself from barking at them. I whipped round to see if Carrie was in a panic and she gave me a scrummy treat.
Horses seem to be very strange creatures to me; they appear to be very flighty and foolish.
Why on earth do they let people sit on them??
I'd bite someone's bum if they did that to me!!

We were walking along and suddenly this thing started running towards us. I was getting ready to shout at it but it turned out to be a leaf blowing in the wind!
I wasn't scared you understand, I just have to be vigilant in case Carrie gets in a tizzy!

When we were a long way from home, we passed by a house where a sassy dog lives and she was up at the fence giving me very plaintive barks and saucy wriggles. I was not going to be seduced away from a tasty liver treat though!!

I then had to sit nicely while Carrie nattered to a friend who stopped in a car. Yack, yack, they went on for ages and just ignored me ... sigh.

We also saw a person with a very pully dog, so Carrie let me hold the ball. That probably wasn't the best idea though as the other dog got REALLY pully then!!
Good job it didn't try to get my ball as I love that ball and don't think I want to share it 😬

Hugs From,
Othello xxx

9th October 2019

I practised putting my two front feet on to lots of different things this morning. What a wag that was, basically getting treats for standing on stuff 😊

Miss Sassy tried to get my attention again while we were walking, but unless she ups her game, I'm still all about the liver treats.

I very much enjoyed Knicker Elastic again today, so Carrie didn't have to count many numbers before I got back to her.

I normally enjoy a good sniff about, but today Carrie had some new treats which I'm partial to so I stayed very close to her.

I've found that just staring up at her when we're walking brings me a lot of those 😂

Her training is looking promising!

Licks from,
Othello xxx

10th October 2019

Me and the gang went out for a walk together this morning as Carrie was in a rush.
So I spent a lot of time this morning fetching the ball back to Carrie, only to have that little wretch, Tofu (he's the Jug), run off with it!!

I can't imagine why she puts up with it!!

One of the terrible terriers spotted something worth chasing, so we all tanked off after it but we didn't get up much steam as Carrie called us and we ran back.
It probably wasn't anything exciting anyway because let's face it, those terriers get excited over fresh air 😂

Carrie forgot my treats, so I had to make do with just strokes … sigh.

Sloppy kisses,
Othello xxx

18th October 2019

Hi From a very wet Wales.

It was very overcast when we set out today, so the farmer's noisy machines had their lights on, but I wasn't bothered.

We saw a lady with her two dogs just in front of us but they were of no interest to me, although they were fascinated by my awesomeness and kept pulling! I just tucked into some nice bits of biscuit that Carrie was drip-feeding me.

Then another dog and its owner appeared from nowhere. I used to get VERY excited about him but I like to keep Carrie calm so I ignored him and got treats.

We played a nice game of ball and Middle.

I kept a close eye on Carrie and she didn't run off today which shows she is learning to behave.

On the way home I saw lots of sheep and they kept running away from the hedge.
I very rarely give their silly behaviour any attention these days 😉

When a child popped out of the bus shelter I thought about barking, but I've seen him before, so I paid no attention and I waited quietly while Carrie chatted to his mother.
I definitely would have considered barking at him in the past, but I'm a good boy now.

Off for a kip now.

Love from,
Othello xxx

22nd November 2019

Hi Guys!

Just dipping my paw back in the waters as we've been away for a while. Carrie was with her extremely sick friend in hospital, and then she was super sad.

We've been playing games as usual and Carrie has been pretty good at staying close, which is a great weight off my mind.

I'm loving Middle so I try to sneak that in whenever there is something that I'm not keen on. Carrie nearly always falls for it and gives me treats (she's such a sucker).

It's been a funny week because some things which normally get me really excited haven't bothered me at all, like our silly cat following us on walks and doing zoomies past us.
Also, the person who is very loud and is always very animated was of no interest to me the other day, so much so that I just turned my back on her and pretended she wasn't there.

However, yesterday the hounds had been through the forest and there were some delicious smells so when we played Knicker Elastic it took me quite a long time to go back to Carrie.
Of course, it was a double whammy for me because I got to do super sniffing and got treats for going back too 😉

I'm glad to say my Super-Power is still working with the treats machine and Carrie is still putty in my paws.

One of Terry's dogs has had puppies and she is really grumpy, so I haven't been allowed to go to his house for "Terry Time" for a couple of weeks.
Carrie says the puppies are cute but of course I know they aren't as cute as me 😁

Anyway, enough for now.

Love to you all,
From your friend,
Othello xxx

24th November 2019

Carrie took me in the car to the park near Terry's house today and I got to see him and Murphy.

Murphy just loves Carrie so much and ignores Terry most of the time when she's there, which Carrie told him is Karma because I've always ignored her when Terry is around 😂

We did lots of running around and catching frisbee then swimming in the river. Most times when Carrie threw the frisbee I took it back to Terry and didn't go to her when she called me (unless she produced the tennis ball, then I loved her best 😂)

I had to walk on the lead for a while because Carrie said I need to be better on the lead around other dogs, as I get a bit excited. I was super good though, so Nah Nah Ne Nah Nah to her 😉

Lucky Murphy got to chase a squirrel while I was on the lead, but Carrie quickly produced the tennis ball, so I didn't try to pull her over to chase it. 😇

This afternoon Carrie and I went for a walk near home and I saw a barking dog. I have to be honest and say I did bark back, but I only barked at it once.

When we met him a bit later on the track, I ignored him because I was fetching the ball which was way more fun.

We played some tug games and I got to chase after Carrie.

Lots of love,
Othello xxx

27th November 2019

I spend a lot of time watching Carrie when we're out on walks.
It's great because I get so many treats 😂
I found that keeping my eye on her really pays off as I'm not having to chase after her so much.

She can be so unpredictable if I'm not watching her!!!!

We were in the forest this morning and I was off the lead when a woman with two dogs came along. Carrie got the ball out and we played fetch while they followed us down the track. Those dogs were especially interested in me, but I was super cool.

This afternoon we played some impulse-control games, which I rather enjoyed because there were two bowls with snacks in. As you know, I like a little snack or two. It was quite exciting because I couldn't guess which bowl Carrie was going to send me to.

We've also been doing some agility. Carrie can be a bit mean with the treats if I don't do things her way, but I reckon I can train that out of her 😂

She is such hard work sometimes … sigh

Bye for now,
Othello xxx

Winter
21st Dec 2019 - 18th Mar
2020

Chapter Three
'A surprise at Christmas'

2nd December 2019

I think Carrie is a bit hacked off with me 😉

Terry came to visit this afternoon and I was soooooo excited.
On reflection, Carrie might have been talking to me but if she did I wasn't hearing her … I love Terry so much 💕

We went for a walk in the forest with him and his two dogs and I mostly just ran by his side gazing up at him and when he threw a stick, I snatched it from whichever dog had it.
I went and lay in a exceptionally dirty puddle too.
I mostly did whatever I wanted and ignored Carrie completely 😊

Carrie put me on the lead for the last part of the walk because she said I was being a thug!! As if!!
I pulled on that lead super hard and I ate sheep poo 😊

Carrie was muttering something like "Get a dog they say, it will be so relaxing, good for your health, lowers your blood pressure". Then she said something about it being a complete crock of bull!

I got the impression that something had annoyed her and I can only imagine it was either Murphy or Bella.

Yours, breathlessly,
Othello xxx

3rd December 2019

Othello here.

I've been angelic today as Carrie seemed to get her knickers in a bunch yesterday after I had such fabulous fun on our walk with Terry 😇

So, every time she stopped walking I gave her a free sit, that seemed to brighten her mood – and I did some very fine Middles too.
I even resisted the temptation to bark back at a dog and I could tell that pleased her.

I've done some smooching up to her as well as she likes that. It doesn't do that much for me but sometimes you just have to put yourself out a bit 😉

Love from,
Othello the angelic xxx

6th December 2019

Omg!! I had a close call earlier!

I was pretty excited when we drew up in the car. I knew exactly where someone had dumped a pile of food, from when we visited the forest the other day.
I remembered but Carrie forgot ... so when we got out of the car I did a nice "sit and stay". Carrie walked off and then called out the release cue.

When she released me, I hurtled towards her, lulling her into a false sense of security, then veered off to get a mouthful of that yumminess.
Sadly, before I even got my mouth on it she called me off ... I was literally about to close my mouth over the first morsel and gulp it down 😔
I have to be honest here, I was imagining the yummy chicken that Carrie might have, or that dumped food what have been scarfed down in the blink of an eye.
I'm so going to have to up my game plan for next time and double back for that food!! 😂

Yours, droolingly,
Othello xxx

11th December 2019

Hi everyone,

I was in kennels over the weekend being spoiled with lots of fuss and treats from the lady I call Auntie Joan.
She likes me and always tells Carrie how well behaved I am.
I rather enjoy my time there.
It doesn't happen very often because Carrie can't bear to be away from me, for obvious reasons, but occasionally she likes to pretend she has a life 😉

The weather has been really stormy here for the last few days, so we haven't been walking in the forest.
We've been playing games indoors and exercising on the treadmill instead.

We had a minor difference of opinion earlier, because it turned out that Carrie hadn't hidden food for ME in the cat biscuit tin – those treats were meant for the cats 😀😀😀

We did go for a little walk along the road yesterday afternoon but the noise and things blowing in the wind really scared me 😔

Carrie gave me treats and took me home quickly, so I could protect the house from the pesky birds by barking at them for stealing food from the bird table.

Lots of love,
Othello xxx

20th December 2019

I am lying here like a good boy on my bed while that silly little Tofu is in the other room barking at the cat coming through the cat flap.
Terriers can be so annoying with their bouncing around and barking. It seems pointless and rather tiring!

To be fair to him, he stopped as soon as Carrie asked him to, but he does like to have his say 😂

I'm a little confused if I'm honest ... yesterday afternoon and this morning I went hunting for treats and found some lovely ones in the composting bin.
I was extremely proud of myself, but Carrie did not seem too impressed 😒
I feel that there needs to be some clarification here as sometimes I'm supposed to feed myself from random items and others I'm not.
There is just no working some people out!!

Your, slightly confusedly,
Othello xxx

21st December 2019

The strangest thing.

Carrie went out earlier and came back with a puppy which apparently is coming to stay for a few days to give its owner a rest.
It's a funny, noisy, little thing
He has tummy ache though, so I suppose he is allowed to complain a bit.

I'm going to reserve judgement on him until I've seen what's in it for me 

Hugs for now,
Othello xxx

24th December 2019

Well, this puppy thing is staying with us now and he is going to be my little brother. We've renamed him Oberon.
I like to call him Little Dude (LD) too.
He had some medicine for his tummy and is now very playful.
If I'd known that having a puppy would mean I got more treats, then I would have seen the value before!
He gets four meals a day and when he gets fed, I get food too

I've been trying to teach him to tug but he's not got the idea yet, although I sense he may be brighter than Carrie.
To set some ground rules, I've been trying to explain that all the toys are mine even if they are both exactly the same.
However, Carrie has different ideas and is getting us to share nicely.

Oberon was much quieter last night.
He slept in his crate quietly until 0200 when he needed a wee and then went back to sleep until 0630.

The two previous nights he was very noisy and needed to toilet loads. At that stage, I was hoping he might turn out to be one of those dogs that people just get for Christmas

I was a much better-behaved puppy, but that will not be a surprise to you 😀

We had some fun rearranging all the blankets on the sofa before having a nap together earlier.

Hope you're having a great Christmas Eve.

Love from,
Othello xxx

25th December 2019

Merry Christmas!!!

Me and the Little Dude, Oberon, have been having fun with our Christmas tuggy 🖤

I'm beginning to see the advantage of having one of these puppy things of my own … extra treats and different games 😂

We also have squeaky toys which are reeeeeallllllly noisy!!
I can tell that everyone in the house likes them because they keep taking them for themselves 😉
Merry Christmas 🖤💕

With much love from,
Othello xxx

27th December 2019

A very odd walk this morning.

We went around a corner and coming towards us was a man with a dog.
Carrie was reactive and made some strange noise because she was surprised, which made me bark.
Fortunately, I soon got the situation back under control by letting her feed me treats 😉

We went on a bit further. I was off the lead in the forest when we came across a woman with two dogs.
They were both on their leads and were doing their pieces.
To add to the bedlam, their owner was shouting at them.
I could see they were really enjoying all the noise, and they barked even more when she joined in!
What a blast they were having 😊

I really hope Oberon does not get that gobby though, as they gave me earache!

We have to time our walks now to coincide with the Little Dude's nap, so I get a good walk and he gets a good sleep.
Otherwise, he'd be a grumpy little bear and those shark teeth of his would be at my ears!

Last night he slept from 2230 until 0700 this morning without needing to toilet which makes up for the few nights disturbed sleep we had 😀

Hugs,
Othello xxx

Chapter Four
'All aboard the rollercoaster'

2nd January 2020 A brief note from Carrie into the online dog training group

As some of you know I had talked myself out of having a puppy, but life has a way of taking our plans and turning them upside down.
Into my life came Oberon, to join Othello and the rest of the crew.
In my wildest dreams I could not have hoped for a better big brother to Oberon than Othello.
Othello has taken to his role like a duck to water. He seems to instinctively know when to encourage the little guy to play with him, particularly when Oberon is being too excitable with his teeth and I'm yipping with pain.
He also clearly gets a lot of pleasure from their games and reverts to being a complete goofball at times but I can very quickly get him to calm down again.
It's early days yet and I know that we will have many ups and downs but I could not be more proud of Othello.💕

Lots of love,
Carrie xxx

4th January 2020

I'm feeling very sorry for myself as I've had to visit the vet this morning.
I have a sore place on my leg and the vet pulled hair out of it to send off for testing while I stood on the table shaking 😞
On the plus side, Carrie gave me loads of treats.
I wasn't bothered by the other dogs in the waiting room and sat quietly while Carrie drip fed me treats.

Apparently, I used to get agitated in the waiting room, but to be honest I suspect it was not me because I'm practically perfect 😂

Knowing her poor memory, she was probably confusing me with one of the Terrible Terriers 😉
I have cream to put on my sore leg. I'll just be licking that off!!

Lots of love,
Othello xxx

7th January 2020

I've been having such fun this morning!

Carrie and I went for a walk and bumped into a lady with a huge dog.
We were both on our leads, so we all went into the forest. He and I had a real blast together.
His owner was a little anxious about him being off his lead with me as he can be a bit excitable sometimes, but it was all fine.
While we were running around together a man came along with another dog so be both tanked off towards them, but Carrie called me back before I got to them 😞
To humour her (and hoping there was a treat in it) I turned round and headed straight back to her, and happily there were lots of treats 😀

We all went our separate ways and then suddenly there were five dogs running towards me and their poor owner was trying to get them all back!!
Of course, I just trotted along by Carrie's side as she was promising me the frisbee. Once we had passed by them, we had a lovely play.

You would think that was enough fun, wouldn't you?

Well, there was more to come in the form of loose sheep!!
Anyway, Carrie was DMTing the heck out of me so I was angelic!

Finally home now; about to have a kip while Oberon is settled.

He is an extremely sad boy whenever he can't be with Carrie – he cries, barks and howls 😢
I hope he grows out of it soon.

Lots of licks,
Othello xxx

8th January 2020

It was the Little Dude's first walk today!

Boy does he like to sniff!! It took an age to walk no distance at all!

Luckily, Carrie said he won't normally come with me.
I think that's because Carrie likes walking me best and does not want to share me.

Went back to the vet this afternoon, and both the nurse and a lady who was there with her dog, said how beautifully behaved I was.
I just sat perfectly staring up at Carrie.

Let's be honest, they really should be more worried about Carrie's behaviour than mine (that's why I had my eye on her) 😉

I didn't even dare look at the other dog, as who knows what Carrie could have got up to in that split second??

Good boy hugs,
Othello xxx

12th January 2020

Sorry I haven't said much for a while.

I haven't had a lot to report as we've been playing games at home and Oberon is very demanding.

Carrie took me and the Little Dude to the kennels for a couple of hours on Friday.
I'm very experienced at it, so Carrie thought Oberon Puck would be comfortable with me there too.
Do you like the addition of Puck as his middle name?
I'm trying it out to see how it fits 😊
We have to go to the kennels sometimes so Carrie can keep up the illusion that she "has a life" ... can't imagine why we can't always go everywhere she goes … sigh.

Anyway, it went very well. Carrie had taken chicken for Auntie Joan to give us while she was away and that was marvellous 😊
When Carrie came back we were both lying in our beds like good boys.

I'm glad to say that she took a divider with her to split the pen. Although I love that dude, I also like my own space.

Lots of love,
Othello xxx

13th January 2020

Oh my days! When we were walking in the forest this morning I was suddenly surrounded by five or six dogs; they came at me from two different directions! Some were barking and one particular dog would not stop sniffing my butt!! Even under that sort of duress, I did not break off from watching Carrie and just ignored them.
I got loads of treats and a great game of ball 

Oberon is being a little viper and keeps snapping at me and stealing my toys from my mouth.
I wonder if Carrie has the receipt so we can exchange him?

Yours, thoughtfully,
Othello xxx

21st January 2019

We went for a nice moochy walk earlier.

The Little Dude stayed at home as he needs to get some rest.

I like to get one walk a day when it's just me and Carrie, but it doesn't always happen.
Being a big brother to Oberon can be extremely hard work!

Anyway, back to the walk.
We were having a game of frisbee when a barky dog came around the corner.
I did give a bark and I was on my way towards him when Carrie called me, so I had to turn on a sixpence and go back.
The woman walking the dog had him on a lead and said he didn't like black dogs, but she still let him come right up to me and stick his nose in my face and butt!!

I was amazingly good and just ignored him because Carrie had my tennis ball in her hand by then (see how well I've trained her?) 😊
The women yacked on for a while and I just sat nicely.
Humans talk about such boring stuff … yawn.

I'm home having a play with the Little Dude now!

Love, as always,
Othello xxx

22nd January 2020

That is what I call a result!!

LD has chosen, for the first time, to go into his crate to sleep!!

Carrie has been working hard on trying to get him to find the crate a nice place.
All sorts of nice treats, that I would have wolfed down, have gone into the crate.
He's had cuddly toys and heat pads, but in the few weeks we've had him he has hated that crate.
Barking and howling whenever he's in it ☹
I used to love my crate, so I don't understand why he gets so sad.

Carrie had a light bulb moment on Monday and moved it to where his raised bed would normally be.
He has chosen to go and sleep in it twice now and settles much more quickly with the door closed.
I'm guessing he won't like it for long though 😉

Your Pal,
Othello xxx

25th January A note from Carrie into the online dog training group

Long post alert!!

The Little Dude, Oberon, is finally sleeping in his crate with the door closed. No whining, barking or howling.

The last month has been a rollercoaster of emotions. I hadn't planned to get another puppy yet but when the little guy needed a home, I just couldn't help myself. He was almost 11 weeks when he came to me and I was his third home – the breeder, his first owner and then me. He's been the toughest of all the pups I've ever had, and I've had a lot (I currently have five dogs and there have been many before them).

To begin with, he barked incessantly when food was around. He also had tummy problems, and I struggled to settle his stomach. He then started to offer signs of resource guarding, which was a new one to me.

I consider myself to be super-tolerant of animals, and patient in their training (not so tolerant of people though 😂) but this little mite almost broke me. I've been reduced to tears of anxiety thinking that my nerves would never stop jangling. I have been feeling guilty that I had "broken" my pack of not-perfect-but-pretty- awesome dogs.

I could not leave Oberon's sight without him having an extreme meltdown, and this was life changing. Just going for a shower was a stressful experience, with me trying to balance out how quickly I could do it with how quickly he would start howling. Trying to get out to walk the other dogs, knowing that he was going to be distressed in his crate, was heartbreaking.

Just thinking about these issues is making me feel stressed now. 😕

House training has been tough too as he just didn't seem to "get it" even though I was using the same methods I'd used successfully with every other dog. His whole demeanour was stressed!

I seriously thought I had made a big mistake in taking him on. However,

through it all, we've had the most beautiful cuddles and those lovely sighs that they do when everything is beginning to become OK in their world.

We've been playing games from day one. We've worked on crate training, and we've worked on life just being less scary.

I think we may have turned a corner and I feel like we're on the path to it all becoming easier. He's only a baby and we've a long way to go but I think that I'm now in familiar territory. He chose to go into Middle yesterday on a walk when another dog scared him.

He sometimes chooses to go to his crate to sleep. He can sometimes tolerate me being out of his sight for miniscule periods of time. He's giving up prized possessions more readily. He's making better choices all round.

I thank my lucky stars every day for Othello, because he is gold. He "gets" the Little Dude and he is so patient with him. He's stepped up as big brother in a way that makes me so proud of him. 💞💞💞💞💞

Lots of love,
Carrie xxx

28th January 2020

We had a nice walk this morning in the sun.
I was allowed to just sniff around with no rules as at all.
Of course, sniffing sometimes leads to eating but we really don't need to go into that 😉

Your buddy,
Othello xxx

Chapter Five
'Othello dips a paw into poetry'

1st February 2020

What a fuss Carrie made this morning when we were out walking!!

The Little Dude came with us, all dressed up in his silly little waterproof outfit 😂😂

Anyway, he did a poo and Carrie made such a fuss that I thought she was having a seizure and I might need to run for help!!
She was dancing around going "niiiice", "good boy", "you star".
Apparently, it's the first one he'd done outside the garden.
It was just a poo!! I've literally done thousands of those!!

I got my own back though as I taught the Little Dude to eat grass and I know that annoys Carrie because I often throw it back up later!!

I'm Carrie's favourite dog as you know, so she usually takes me out by myself.
She takes the Little Dude by himself too, but that's just so he doesn't get jealous of how well behaved I am 😉

While we were out today, we saw those mouthy dogs again.

I can tell you that if Oberon ends up that gobby I'm going to disown him! They do my swede in!!

I considered jumping in some super muddy ditches, but before I could make my mind up Carrie was scattering food around and I got distracted.
Worry not though because I know exactly where they are 😂

Before she took me out walking again, Carrie was trying to teach Boundary Games to Little Dude but he is completely useless at them. He's way too interested in my treats, so Carrie was having to DMT him away.
To be honest, Don't Make Trouble has his name all over it!!

Lots of love,
Othello xxx

2nd February 2020

More crazy behaviour from Carrie, just because the Little Dude did a poop in the forest!!

Played a good game though. Carrie threw the frisbee for me and when the squirt started to follow me, she called him back.
He had 100% success at it which meant I got the frisbee to myself every time 😂
It's not that I don't like sharing it's just that he runs off with it because he doesn't understand the importance of playing properly.
Frisbee is a very serious game and in my opinion it's just not for babies.
When he gets a bit bigger I can just body slam him out of the way but he's a real tittle tattle at the moment, and if I accidentally bump him, he cries like he's being murdered ... sigh.

He also rushes to get into Middle so that he gets the first treat, so I have to be super careful not to tread on him!!

However, he did a great job of vomiting up that grass in the night, so I was pleased with yesterday's lesson.

He also ate a slug earlier, something I would never do, but you've got to admire him for giving it a go.

Bye for now,
Othello xxx

2nd February 2020 a poem by Othello

I sometimes sit and wonder why
She had to get the little guy?
He steals my toys and makes me sigh
I really wonder, why-oh-why?

He'll sometimes bark, or cry, or howl
Enough to make an angel scowl
I wonder, did she make a mistake?
Or will he soon be my best mate?

He likes to sleep on her knee
Sometimes really close me
I'm trying to care for Little Dude
Although, not enough to share my food

Over all, I think he's neat
Even when he nips my feet
We're trying to make him really happy
Our funny, cheeky, little chappy.

5th February 2020

The Little Dude may be a bit of a whiner, BUT boy can he get back to Carrie quick!
He's making my selective hearing a bit obvious!

I'm going to do my best to stop him being such a goodie-two-shoes!!

Carrie took him to the park today and he was off the lead playing with another pup but stopped immediately when she called him.
He also ran straight back to her from a bicycle and several other loose dogs.

Apparently, he did a wee there too (so what??) and hardly whined at all.

I know all this because I heard Carrie on the phone saying how good he was.

I've been super well behaved as usual. I've had some nice chews and a really good game of fetch in the garden while Oberon was napping in his crate.

By the way, the terrible terriers and Truffles completely wrecked a frisbee they were supposed to fetch when Carrie was playing with them in the field.
They are so naughty and I love it, 'cos they make me look sooo good! 😂😂😂

Lots of love,
Othello xxx

9th February 2020

Well, what a crazy day of wind and rain!

We've been having a blast playing games indoors and finally the Little Dude has learnt to lie down when he's asked.
It's difficult to tell if he's really clever or really stupid sometimes 😕

I'm looking forward to more fun as Carrie has taken up the carpet protector, because she reckons the Little Dude is reliable enough not to have accidents now.
I think she's forgotten that the meds he's on for his tummy upset him, so I can see trouble ahead 😂😂😂😂😂

Carrie put all our toys through the dishwasher and our cuddlies in the washing machine yesterday, so they all taste disgusting now.
It's going to take an age to get them back to a suitable state, so the clean smell has gone 😶

I think you'll remember that I thought LD's little waterproof outfit a little ridiculous, well now I think it's hilarious because he finds really stinky puddles to jump in and the coat gets full of dirty water.
It's great because Carrie gets super excited and then LD jumps up at her … it's just a joy to watch.

I had no paw in teaching him about puddles and ditches you understand 😜
However, I may have helped him to find the best places to find horse poo.
I consider that a brotherly duty and I know he appreciates it 😀

There's been fun with toys today, as well as lots of tug games.
I snuck a game of tug with LD earlier, but I don't think Carrie appreciated us taking the stuffing out of the toy for some reason???

Yesterday Carrie was having one of her "odd" days and she kept running off.
LD and I had our work cut out keeping our eyes on her!!

Best that you all stay safe indoors today if you can as it's very windy!

Love from,
Othello xxx

10th February 2020

Morning from Othello!

There are a lot of trees lying down in the forest today. Carrie said it was because of the windy weather.
It's great though because it makes for fun trying to find a way around them.
They are also great for walking along and jumping over, just like agility really 😊

Carrie told me that she was Super Proud of me today because I completely ignored five dogs which charged up to me.
I just ran to her and sat waiting for her to throw me the frisbee, even when one of the little dogs was humping me!
The lady with the other dogs said I was gorgeous, which of course I am 😂

A little while later I did the same when we met a man with his dog.
Carrie and he chatted for a while and I even ignored his treats.

We got back home before the torrential rain came but Carrie had to go and play with the other dogs in the field.
LD and I decided to wait indoors and stay warm and dry 😀

Stay safe everyone!!

Hugs and licks,
Othello xxx

13th February 2020 Carrie into the online dog training group

Progress!!

I left the room with the door open and went to the kitchen to get a drink of water. When I came back I found Oberon (aka LD) still on his bed. He

wagged his tail at me but still stayed where he was!! He's moved now and is lying with his head on my foot, which I rather like.

Lots of love,
Carrie xxx

Morning!

I've been acting dumb over the Cone game for months now.
To be honest, I was happy just looking at the Cone and getting a treat for it 😂

LD played it for the first time and only went and stuck his nose in it after just a few goes.
You could have knocked me down with a feather because this is the little guy who is scared of everything.
I have to be totally honest and say that I'm more than a little disappointed in him.

Of course, I had to up my game then and stick my flipping nose in it.
I really don't think he understands that we have to get Carrie to work for the reward of us doing something!!!
If he takes his eye off his chew later it's going to be history!!

Lots of love,
Othello xxx

16th February 2020

Carrie said it's not safe to walk in the forest today because of the wind so we've been playing indoors.

My favourite game was the "rip the stuffing out of the toys" game that LD and I played while Carrie was making a row with her guitar.

If we made that sort of noise, we'd be put in time out 😏

Carrie instigated a few games including Middle, Boundary Games and Mouse. She's trying to persuade LD to not bark every time he and I play, but she's having no success there at all 😂😂😂

I'm currently trying to mug her pockets for treats by sitting really close to her on the sofa.

I've taught LD a really good game in the garden which gets him into trouble. I call it the "rummage in the borders for cat presents" game 😂😂😂
We both think it's a fantastic way of entertaining ourselves with a good chance of winning a prize at the end 😉
It's also funny to see Carrie making those gagging noises 😀😀

Slobbery kisses,
Othello xxx

19th February 2020

More rain so we didn't get very long walks today but still got soaked!

I feel as if I've accomplished a lot with LD because he now runs back and forth in puddles, getting his silly coat filthy.

Once we'd dried off, we played games in the house.

LD's growing very quickly so I'm pleased to say that he is able to reach things from much higher up now. I get to play with things that I'm not normally allowed, and everyone knows he took them.
I could reach these things myself of course but I'm not going to risk being told off 😂

Lots of love,
Othello xxx

20th February 2020

I simply will not lie on my boundary properly because Carrie is trying to starve me to death and I can hardly lift my paws to get onto it.
She says it's because I've got an upset tummy, but I don't see how that matters. LD was allowed food earlier, even though he scarfed down a bone from some rotting animal he found in the forest. Grrr ...

I assure you I will be sharing my very ripest parps for the rest of the day and I may very well insist on going outside in the middle of the night.
I'm always impressed how fast Carrie can move if I jump off the bed and whine 😂

Yours, with a rumbly tumbly,
Othello xxx

22nd February 2020 A note form Carrie into the online dog training group

I'm sorry for another post but I can't help myself because I am so proud of Othello!!

Rewind to August last year and if I had been walking Othello and we had come across this particular person and their barking dog I would have come out in a cold sweat knowing that Othello would be barking and pulling. I would literally be hanging into his lead and digging my heels in whilst praying that he didn't pull me over. Fast forward to today and I'm not only walking him, but I have LD with me, we're on the road and there is literally nothing to do but keep walking towards them.

So, I just took a deep breath, said to myself "You have sooooo got this" and reached into my pouch for a tuggy with a ball on it. LD barked at the other dog in an excited puppy way and Othello just looked at me and the tuggy without even changing pace.
We just walked on by and I exchanged pleasantries with the other dog's owner.
I could have cried with pride at my Super Star boy. Obviously, he got the tuggy, loads of calm praise and when we got home a heap of chicken.

Lots of love,
Carrie xxx

25th February 2020

I've been having a blast messing with Carrie's head this morning 😂😂

**She wanted to play Boundary Games with LD and me, but she wasn't telling me what I was supposed to do so I took the opportunity to act dumb.
LD was being a right goodie-two-shoes and getting onto his raised bed without being asked.**

**I thought I would put a spanner in the works and and chase his treats too ... LOL, it was Crazyville for a while.
I did stop in the end and stay on my raised bed, but when she gave me the release cue and threw a treat, I didn't always get back on 😂😂😂
I did see my error in the end though, because LD hopped back on every time and was getting treats!!**

Then she played Middle and Mouse with LD, so I did stay on my bed.

**When she tried to do them with me, LD kept going into Middle 😂😂
We thought it was really funny, but I think Carrie's head was spinning.**

She normally plays games with us separately but today was even more fun!!

LD started off today being quiet but, sadly he's gone all barky again.

Big hugs,
Othello xxx

<u>28th February 2020 – Oberon finds his voice</u>

Ello itz Oberon here, although I fink I iz best known to u az Wickle Dude, az dat iz wot mys big bwuvver Thello calls I. He also sometimes has uvver names for I dat he sez wewy quietly under his breath 😏
He iz mys hero and wen I gwow up I iz going to be just wike im 😀🖤

Dis being a puppy stuff iz ard work, ticularly wen u ave a person wike Cawwie in your life!!
She iz gweat at cuddles and tug though. Thello warned I that she waz slow to catch on wen I arrived but I never spected her to be quite so difficult.

Take dis morning for winstance ...

Every morning she finks she iz cweeping out of bed wivout waking I az I iz snoozing in mys cwate. WRONG! I ear her get up and I iz quite snuggly with mys wuverly eat pad, so I iz appy to stay in bed a wickle bit longer.
But dis morning I fort she waz making I wait a bit long, so I frew in a few wickle owls to get her attention.
I wud ave oped for a quicker reaction weally but she didnt come til after I stopped owling!! Crazy eh??
Now dat iz a bit mutch az I iz only a baby and we babiez arent spposed to be patient.
We look dis cute so everyone bendz to our needz and wantz 😄
Anyway, I did mys wee in de garden and she did her funny

dance (she never used to do dat dance wen I peed on de wug 😏)
At dis point mys tummy iz a wumbling so I iz charging around and virtually pointing at de fridge door, but she cides to ave a cup of tea!! ow mutch clearer did I needz to be??
Wen de penny finally dwopped I waz weak with unger, she gave I food weally slowly and made diculous noisez.
After dat I ad to make wike de waised bed was a gweat place to be before I got any more food.
Just wen I fort she was getting de point, I would ave to leap off de bed and get a morsel of food ... It waz wewy tiring.

On Monday she took I to dis odd place dat we ad visited de week before and just left I der!! The lady was nice to I but she did weally odd stuff with mys fur and even gave I a shower and stuck I under a warm windy fing (Cawwie ad sent chicken wiv I so I got lots of dat witch waz nice though).
While I was der I honed mys barking skills and now dey are perfected and I iz showing dem off to everyone and everyfing I comes across.
I ave to say I iz wewy proud of iself 😀 I weckon I ave got de bark of a mutch more gwown up boy.
I iz not sure dat Cawwie haz de right ear to preciate it though az sadly I iz not getting the praise I deservz.
I also learned to hump while I was der and I az been practising that too.
Thello got weally gwumpy wiv I yesterday evening wen I shared it wiv im.
I fort he and Cawwie would both enjoy mys affection but dey didnt.

It iz waining ard here again so I iz tending on sitting on Cawwie's knee and gazing into her eyes coz I wuv her.🖤🖤

Wuv U 

29th February 2020

Morning Lovely People!

Boy Carrie has got a short fuse this morning!

Apparently, we are not allowed to play tug with Otter until his stuffing falls out!!

I know what you are thinking "She's just crazy and unreasonable" and you'd be right!

We've un-stuffed Rabbit and Beaver before and Pheasant and Road Kill, so I don't know why she's gone all "only tuggies are for tugging" this morning.
I'm not even allowed to get LD's Hippo or Leopard out of the box!!

I think she should be a little kinder to me as I had to get up four times in the night with my upset tummy.
All she had to do was follow me around with an umbrella a torch, poo bags and disinfectant.

I've been on yucky medicine in case I've got the nasty that thing that LD had.
Furthermore I got no breakfast!!

Love from a very sad,
Othello xxx

Cawwie waz virtually doing cartwheels dis morning coz I ad firm poo!! 😁😁😁

Dont mention it to Cawwie but Thello and I iz playing tug wiv a gardening glove 😁
I az got mys eye on a fluffy cushion but I iz not quite tall enuff yet.
Der will be so mutch fun wen I can weach it though!

Thello az two of de fingers from de glove in iz mouth but I will quickly kick dat under de sofa. No harm done 😋

I understandz Calmness and Boundary Games are going to be played soon but not til Cawwie az drunk more tea.
She iz looking a bit ragged around de edges today so I fink I will sing de Cockapoo tribal song to her later 😁😁

Wuv U
🐾

Spring
19th Mar – 19th Jun
2020

Chapter Six
'Frog spawn, a vole and little O'

1st March 2020

We went deep into de woods off de tracks and I waz running and falling and splashing in puddles.
Der waz so many new smells and fings to climb on and under, so I ad to shout mys excitement out loud.
We played a lot of Race back to Middle but der waznt mutch room for both of us, so Thello trod on I a few times but I waz wewy brave about it.
Cawwie was throwing frisbee for Thello and wen I followed im she would call I back for a treat. I iz wewy good at dat but her treats are getting a bit boring so I may stop til she gives I chicken 😁

Before we went out we played Boundaries but silly Cawwie forgot to tell I dat I could get off so I waz left sat by iself on mys bed.

I ave found a wewy interesting place to ave a dig by de door in de lounge and I fink if I works ard over the next few days I could pull de carpet up so Cawwie can vacuum under it 😁

Wuv U

I took LD to the river this morning, but he wouldn't get in when I did.

I'm going to keep practising with him though because I know Carrie loves it when I go swimming and I get the car wet inside.

Thankfully, I haven't found any fox poo recently but when I do I'll share it with Little Dude as he's got really good fur for it 😉 I wouldn't want it in my fur but I can see some fun to be had 😉

My tummy is feeling better today, and I managed to get a good night's sleep.

It's gone all rainy again now so I'm glad we're back in the warm.

Lots of love,
Othello xxx

2nd March 2020

It's been a real blast here as Carrie bought us lots of new toys to investigate.

I've no idea why Carrie stuffed food into rubber snakes, but one way or another I'm going to get it out 😉

LD was very brave and stuck his head a paper bag to get some food, which was a bit disappointing as I was hoping for leftovers.

We had a stonking walk this morning and got loads of treats.
We kept diving off into the woods for a rummage which made Carrie call us back.
Both of us raced back and squeezed into Middle.
LD was racing off to eat something delicious at one point, but he did come straight back. I would have found it really funny if he'd got to it and rolled in it!

I was rather hoping that while Carrie was whooping at him I could sneak in and snaffle it up but, alas, she appeared to have eyes in the back of her head.

Sloppy licks,
Othello xxx

Thello has stolen mys bed so I ave ad to ave a snooze in mys cwate (wiv de door open or I wud cwy)

When I got up dis morning and went outside for a wee mys eyes hurt and I ad to squiz dem up coz it waznt dark and cloudy or waining.
It waz also funny on our walk coz the sky az gone blue and goes on forever.
I took your advice and I didnt do any singingin in mys cwate yesterday but I did do some on our walk.

Wuv U

<u>4th March 2020</u>

Thello sez I ave too mutch to say, so I az to talk less!
I ad a nice play in de woods today although I waz a bit worried dat a tiny bear might be hiding and waiting to eat I, so I did quite a lot of barking to scare it off.
I never saw one so I finks it worked 😊

Wuv U

A note from Carrie into an online dog training group

My cup truly runneth over today. I took Oberon to a café, being pretty certain that he would have a meltdown. On the last two occasions we've been he's whined and barked. We met Terry and his pup outside to try to keep energy levels low.
As we stepped inside, immediately a child screamed. Needless to say, LD barked, which was a reasonable reaction. We sat down and I drip fed him his lunch and gave him a filled KONG™. Astonishingly there was not a peep out of him. It was a different café from the one we visited before, but it was busy with lots of noise and young children. Amazingly, I drank my tea in peace and quiet!
So, feeling refreshed, we went for a run in the park with Terry's dogs. Oberon gave his two older dogs a wide birth as he was anxious of them, but played with his pup. He got covered in mud from playing so much and then surprised me by jumping into the river with Terry's dogs. A definite result as he came out much cleaner.

That is what I call a win!

Lots of love,
Carrie xxx

Apparently, I am a very good boy and to prove it I got lots of treats.

While we were walking in the forest, three dogs came piling up to me, so I just sat by Carrie's side gazing up at her and my much-loved frisbee.
The other dogs were getting very personal with their sniffing and one of them, who had a squashed face, got right up into my face so I did do a little grrrr at him, but I stayed staring at Carrie.
I think I exhibited great self-control really. Humans wouldn't like it if strangers came right up to their face like that!

We went a little further on and played some more frisbee and then SIX dogs ran up to me!
I was a bit surprised to be honest, but I know that I have to offer a calm presence these days 😉
I went into my good boy sit and stayed there while Carrie chatted to their owners.
The man said that I am the PERFECT LABRADOR because I'm so well behaved and sat nicely even when his dogs were sniffing at me.
I could see that Carrie was Super Proud of me.

When we got home there was a man delivering to our house, but I just ignored him and then got to play ball and had a big handful of treats.

Unfortunately, Oberon was barking and howling in his crate because the man knocked on the door.

Doggy sighs,
Othello xxx

6th March 2020

Hi Everyone

We've had fun today as we had "Terry Time" and six of us dogs went for a walk with him.
I think Carrie came too. Who knows though? I was hanging out with my bestie 😊
He threw sticks for us and we went in lots of mud and did jumping in ditches and charging around.
Actually, I remember Carrie was there because she had a ball and I was interested in her then 😂
She got it out when there was a little girl with a bag of crisps ... I can't imagine why though 😂

Lots of love,
Othello xxx

LD here
I did try to join in a bit wiv de big dogs but some of dem growled at I, so I mostly stayed wiv Cawwie coz I weally like her best.
Thello didnt play with I at all.
I got wewy, wewy, muddy so I ave just ad a bath.
I ad lots of treats for coming back straight away.

Wuv U

7th March 2020

Morning!

We had a very muddy walk this morning with lots of new smells in the forest. It was a bit frustrating for me though because LD was barking at everything. When he stopped Carrie gave us both a treat which was nice but we didn't progress our walk very fast … sigh.

I picked up the smell of something really delightful at one point and went off to find it with LD. A bit reluctantly we went back when Carrie called us.

Tomorrow, I will try a extra stealthy approach to it as it will be even tastier by then 😊 and very possibly worth rolling in 😂

I did get my ball for going back to Carrie. When I dropped it at her feet LD ran

off with it though, little wretch.
I was a bit disappointed with that outcome as I love that ball and I don't want him stealing it.
Anyway, Carrie got it back and distracted him with a bit of Middle so I could have a play with it.
There were loads of those two-wheeled growling and roaring machines on the tracks which don't bother me but I imagine you can guess what LD did. Yep, bark, bark, bark!!!

I'm having a bit of fun with Carrie pretending that I don't like the new crate in the car so that I get treats to get in 😂😂

My aim today is to try and remove the stuffing from one of the new soft toys we got.
I had a go earlier but got caught in the act!!
Have a good day everyone.

Your friend,
Othello xxx

Oberon here.
I ad lots of fun in de mud and de puddles today and came home smelling weally gorgeous.
I ave been trying to train Cawwie to give I more treats by barking a lot.
Turns out barking doeznt get I treats 😕
I tried to play wiv Thellos ball. Neither he or Cawwie seemed to want to share it wiv I, witch I fink is wewy mean 😟
I iz looking forward to a cuddle with Cawwie once I az dried off and den some nice games later.
Puppy hugs and kisses 😘

8th March 2020 Carrie into the online dog training group

Today Oberon is having a challenging day! So much insane barking on our walk this morning. 😟 At lunchtime I popped him into his crate with a delicious filled KONG, so we could have our meal in peace and he went into a full blown howling fest and ignored his KONG.
Poor Othello will be demanding ear plugs soon.
I tried some Boundary Games with Oberon, but he was predicting the release cue and bouncing off his bed every few seconds. I obviously need to be more careful with my body language 😔 When we went into the garden to do a bit of DMTing, he thought cat poop was worth hunting for. Othello is going to regret teaching him that trick, as LD is much faster than him!
I must remember not to let him snuggle too close later when he wants his evening cuddle!!
Sigh …
Tomorrow is another day …

Lots of love,
Carrie xxx

9th March 2020

We went to town this morning and firstly walked around the park with me on my lead.
That was unusual as we normally play frisbee there, so I was a bit unsure of what was going to happen.

LD waited in the car.

Then we walked into the town centre where they were people and a few dogs.

Carrie gave me my ball quite a lot for ignoring distractions, which was cool.
I'm not keen on towns at all as I'm not used to all the busy stuff.

I think I wasn't the best of boys at one point though. There were two Labradors in the back of a parked trailer, and they were barking like crazy at me.
I even tried to pull Carrie across the road so I could shout back at them … whoops!

After a bit more walking, we went into a cafe (I've never been in one of those before) and that was brilliant as Carrie brought yummy KONGS and rubber mats with squashed food in for me to lick.
I just licked and chewed while she and the woman were yacking on.

I did bark a couple of times at a child that kept running close to me and then stopping and staring at me!
I'm guessing he'd never seen such a handsome, well behaved, dog before 😀😀😀 but I stopped barking when Carrie gave me some treats.

I was rather hoping that some food might fall off one of the trays that was being carried around.
It did cross my mind that with a bit of a nudge I could have lightened those trays for the ladies 😏

Slobbery kisses,
Othello xxx

Oberon here.
I got out of de car in de park and Thello got back in.
I walked and I barked.
Den I barked and I walked.
Den I got back in de car.
It waz a real blast az I wuv barking.

14th March 2020

I've been staring at Carrie in a very concerned way.

Some of you will remember the incident where she smacked herself in the face with a weight.
Well, I think the head injury is back with a vengeance.

Oberon and I were having a perfectly lovely walk, when all of a sudden she started calling out strange things and waving to people I couldn't see or hear.
She was acting like a crazy lady!
"Good morrow fair fellow" then "Fabulous, next Friday would be great" and the like.
This was worth a bark in my opinion, but I have no idea at what??
We stuck right by her side after she'd done that a few times as I seriously thought she was having an episode (again).
I'm wondering whether it's a way of tricking us into ignoring people at the door?

Prior to her odd behaviour we'd been mooching around off track in the woods.
I almost got to investigate and unstuff the remains of a bird, but she spotted me 😟

Then I dashed into the river but got called out again. I was a bit miffed about that! It ended well though because I showed LD how to lie down in a muddy puddle and he loved it 😂😂
He got his little waterproof coat super mucky ..."You're very welcome" I said 😀
We couldn't really go very far as Carrie kept running off and hiding if we looked away.
LD gets a bit worried if he can't see her and I have to look out for him 😀
He was in fine voice this morning, charging around and barking like a little bark monster 😂😂😂
Have a good weekend 💜

Your friend,
Othello xxx

I ran in de woods and I barked.
Den I barked and ran in de woods
Den I lay in some mud.
Den went home.
It was fab!

Wuv U

16th March 2020

Have been to town today to meet up with one of Carrie's friends.

I played frisbee with them in the park,
Apparently, there were lots of other dogs and lots of noisy children. I didn't notice any of them because I was having so much fun 😊

Carrie and her friend took LD for a little walk in the park and I sat in the car and watched.
I heard him barking. He said it was because there was a loud noise, but I think he likes the sound of his own voice!

Lots of love,
Othello xxx

17th March 2020

Carrie has been playing Two Paws On with us.
I have tried to think of where I would implement this game. My best option would be sneakily reaching for the cat food on their climbing frame.

I was a little distracted when it was my turn because LD was whining in the other room.

We have some new blocks to put our paws on but they're a bit wobbly.
I will persevere with them though, as you never know when new skills will come in useful.

I could see LD through the door when he was doing it and he kept lying down with his paws on the blocks ... lazy boy 😂

Carrie has been talking a lot about people panic-buying food because of something called Corona Virus.
I'm going all weak thinking they might run out of my food ... gulp.

Slobbery kisses,
Othello xxx

Played.
Ad treats.
Stopped playing.

Wuv U

19th March 2020

Today I allowed Carrie to be more exciting than a cat that ran across the road in front of us 😂😂
She seemed very distracted at the time so I weighed it up and thought I'd just ignore it.
I sense that these little wins mean a lot at the moment and the tasty treat went down very well so it was worth it 😏

We had to go out in the car earlier and just as we were being loaded in a huge bird swooped down and snatched a dove.

I'm fond of most little animals so it was a sad incident, the poor little thing was screeching, but we were good boys and didn't make any fuss.

Sniffs,
Othello xxx

Oberon here.
Wuv Two Feet On.
Nuffin else to say.
But ...

Wuv U 

<u>20th March 2020</u>

I walked.
Waz barked at by a dog behind a fence.
I did not bark.
Cawwie spoke to man on other side of road for AGEZ.
I did sit wewy nicely.
Dog behind fence barked.
I did not bark.
I got treats and den more treats.
Went home.

Wuv U 

21st March 2020

The sun is shining and it's a beautiful day for a swim in a lovely green, slimy, pond 😂
I'm not entirely sure why Carrie was making those funny noises after I did it, but my guess is that it was in appreciation of how lovely I smell 😀

I smell so much nicer than LD now, he came home yesterday smelling all flowery which was very odd as no one in their right mind could possibly like that more than a nice bit of pond scum??????😂

I played some Two Paws On, Middle and Knicker Elastic.

Stay safe and well everyone.

Love you lots,
Othello xxx

Yesterday went to gwoomer.
Barked and whined wen it hurt.
Did not bark or whine wen it did not hurt.
I got treats.
Cawwie sez I smell nice.
I will change dat soon.
Did not see many people.
Went to cafe with Cawwie and Jo.
Chewed a chew.
Did not bark or whine.
Came home.

Wuv U

22nd March 2020 Othello's wise words concerning Corona Virus

I sense the madness all around
So have some sense and go to ground!
Things just aren't quite the same
But we'll feel better with a game😀

Did Two Paws On.
Got a treat.
Wike treats.

Wuv U

23rd March 2020 Carrie into the online dog training group

I took Oberon for a 10 minute leg stretch around the village and I am more interesting than a dog in a garden barking at us, and then another dog barking at us!!
Progress is being made!

Lots of love,
Carrie xxx

I'm appealing to you for help today.

Please could you explain to Carrie that asking me to catch my food when LD is in the room just isn't fair?
I can't help it if she's a useless thrower. When I miss LD hoovers up MY food!!

She normally puts him somewhere else when we're training, but he's being a big baby today, so she let him stay.

I'm usually very understanding and very tolerant of his needy behaviour.
Let's face it he's taking the heat off anything I'm up to when he's got her attention 😊

She can't be expecting me to work for my food if he's sitting on her knee.

Today though, I feel positively weak with hunger 😟😂
I've been giving him the evils out the corner of my eye but he thinks it's a new game and keeps licking my ears.

From your saintly friend,
Othello xxx

<u>24th March 2020</u>

The sun's shining and it was lovely to play ball and Middle this morning!
The river was a bit chilly but how would I know that if I didn't test it out?

There are so many people at home so it was nice to get out for a little while, before the rain comes again.
Although to be honest I like it when there are lots of muddy puddles to lie in.
Mud is extremely good for my skin and fur. That's how I keep it so shiny 😀

There isn't much frog spawn in the ditches at the moment which is a shame as Carrie loves it when I come out covered in it 😂

We saw a sheep and a cute lamb and I did pull towards them but then I remembered that I don't do that anymore 😂

Lots of love,
Othello xxx

I az been sitting.
I az watching.
I did no barking.
I saw sheep.
I did bark.

Wuv U

25 March 2020

Did not bark at airdryer.
Did eat some scatter feed by iself.
Not scared of agility tunnel.
Wuv jumping.

Wuv U

25th March Carrie into the online dog training group

For anyone who doesn't know Oberon these are HUGE events!
He came to me at 11 weeks old, just before Christmas, with more anxieties than any dog should have in several lifetimes 😟 Since he went to the groomer a month ago, he's had a meltdown every time I've used the hairdryer and he's barked at it like crazy.
He has never eaten without me by his side or very close. Today I left the

room for a very short time, without him giving up on his food and following me. The agility tunnel would previously have been super, super, scary but today he coped brilliantly, even though he hadn't seen it before. As far as having toys in a box is concerned, just having a box in the room was a freak out event. Now he EATS food from the toy box, puts two feet in it and just loves to steal the items and play with them. He has also managed to pass barking dogs and not react. He still suffers from Separation Anxiety, but we are making steady progress. Sometimes I can leave him for a few seconds in a different room and even, occasionally, for a few minutes.

Please remind me of this post when I am despairing next time

Lots of love,
Carrie xxx

I have been very helpful today by hoovering up every scrap of my scatter feed and helping Carrie with her workout 😂😂
My intentions today are to act dumb in order to get as many treats as possible, and to elbow LD out of the way when we play catch.

Lots of love,
Othello xxx

26th March 2020

I did bark at dog dat barked at I.
I did play in mud.
I did play Middle and Two Paws on.
I did not bark at sheep.
Did not see any sheep 😉
I did not bark at horses.

Did not see any horses 😉
Did play Knicker Elastic.
Did not see any Knicker Elastic 😉

Wuv U

Morning!

Today I felt like a little bit of mischief, so I had a lovely swim 😀
The particular swimming hole I chose leaves my fur a rather nice shade of chocolate brown 😏

I also did a little bark at a silly horse that popped its head up from behind a bush (that was funny because it made Carrie jump 😂😂)
I seriously considered rolling in some frog spawn which was drying up on the path, but I felt it might compromise the benefits of my mud bath.

We played lots of games and some ball.
My tummy is full and I'm ready for a snooze.

Snoozy hugs,
Othello xxx

<u>27th March 2020</u>

Today we have been practising Leg Weaves but I feel that any errors are solely down to the person in charge of the treats. I tried to rise above it though 😂

Love from,
Othello xxx

I weaved.
I got treats.
I iz clever boy.

I az been lying wewy still and Thello az been poking I.
He is twying to get I into twouble.
I did not do nuffin, an I iz sticking to dat story.

Wuv U

LD is trying to get me into trouble.
He started it and when Carrie looked at us he just lay still and played at cute!!?

Lots of love,
Othello xxx

Carrie here
Today I have already been more alluring than cat poo!
We all know how alluring that makes me. 😉

Lots of love,
Carrie xxx

29th March 2020

Today I have poo on my mind and I'm not sure that it's making Carrie happy, but I don't see why.
A boy has to pass his time somehow doesn't he? 😂

While she was playing with LD I thought I would be helpful and clear up in the flower borders for her.
Those cats are very untidy 😂😂
I was hoping for some thanks and I felt it was unnecessary for her to make those gagging noises and send me indoors!

I kind of felt that perhaps I'd misunderstood this tidying up stuff, so I tried to make up for it.
My inspiration came from remembering that yesterday, when she was cuddling me, she said I was a bit smelly and needed a bath (very rude!!).
So, I thought I would take matters into my own hands and save her the hassle of bathing me.
When she was ahead of me on our walk, I had just the tiniest little shoulder-dipping rub in some bird poo to improve my smell.
Talk about over-react!! Off she went again with the gagging noise!!

Sometimes I am just clueless about what she wants??

On the plus side, the games we've been playing today give treats for just following her around. This is great, particularly for LD 'cos he's like her shadow anyway.

Your delicious-smelling friend,
Othello xxx

30th March 2020

I felt, after not allowing Carrie to be more interesting than poo yesterday, I should cut her some slack.
Of course, this has nothing to do with me enjoying treats 😏😂

So, today I allowed her to be more appealing than Twts (Tuts). He's one of the cats that sleeps in our house.
He followed us up the road and I did my best ignoring-things behaviour 😉
This of course meant I got a few little snacks to take the edge off my hunger pangs 😀
Just to get me even more points I ignored Twts with his freshly caught vole 😂😂😂😂

Twts likes to come with us and saunter around waving his tail to try to tempt me to chase him, but I don't do things like that anymore 😏😏
I'm such a good boy.

Love from,
Othello xxx

Can put two paws on.
Did put two paws on.
Can bark at people.
Did not bark at people.
Can bark at dog.
Did not bark at dog.
Did owl in cwate wen Cawwie went outside.

Wuv U

31st March 2020

I am very tired from being so well behaved ... yawn.

I have been helping with LD's training today and I showed him some basic survival skills as I'm worried dog food supplies may run low.
My first lesson was on how to increase energy levels by attempting to eat some stuff from the kitchen bin.

I heard that the men who empty the bins might not be coming as often so I was also being helpful.

Needless to say, my intentions were misunderstood

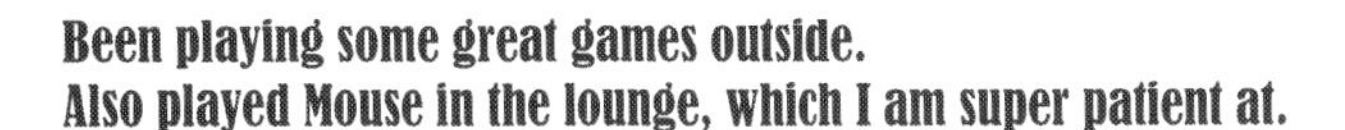

Been playing some great games outside.
Also played Mouse in the lounge, which I am super patient at.

Sloppy kisses,
Othello xxx

Wike games.
Could not weach bin.
Did bark.

Chapter Seven
'Ground delights and eyebrow frights'

2nd April 2020

Did you hear me singing "lalalalala"?
I bet you did because I have been singing it in my head very loudly!! 😂
Carrie, who let's face it is a bit dim sometimes, forgot (!!) to take LD to the bathroom with her while she had her shower and for some ridiculous reason left him in his pen.
He decided to go into full blown howling and my poor ears were stinging.
I took myself as far away as possible, but I could still hear him!!
My poor, poor, ears!!

Next time I'm going to cover them, so they're paw paw ears (get it?) 😂😂

Hugs,
Othello xxx

Got left alone.
Barked.
Owled.

Not wike.
Sad.

Shhhh…More about I az Thello iz asleep 😉
I did play in mud.
I did ave bath.
I did bark at airdwyer.
Stopped.
Got treats.
Did not bark at airdwyer.
Finished treats.
Barked at airdryer.

3rd April 2020

I woke up and found biscuits by my snout.
This leads me to believe that the snack fairy came. I like this concept 😂
As I have heard about concept training does this mean I have trained the snack fairy?
Does this make me a qualified fairy trainer? 😉

Slobbery kisses,
Othello xxx

Oberon here.
Saw dogs.
Did not bark.
Dogs barked at I.
I did bark.
Dogs barked more.
I did not bark.
I got treats.
I did owl in playpen.

Wuv U

Itz I again.
I ave magic wike Othello.
I can make treat machine give I treats.
I iz a big boy now.

Wuv U

4th April 2020

We took LD with us today, so I had competition to get back to Carrie first.

At one point I found something really tasty on the ground, so I was a bit slow to race back but it was worth it because I got yummy ground delights and treats 😂😂

Later on in the walk we found horse poo and I suggested LD try it 😂😂
Carrie didn't see me eat any so that obviously means that I didn't.
Not seen, no foul 😂

Love from,
Othello xxx

I does Wuv mud and it must Wuv I too coz it sticks to mys fur for agez.

<u>5th April 2020 Carrie into online dog training group</u>

Happy 4th Birthday to Othello!! Always the Sunshine in my life! A bit challenging, but in the best possible way. He waited for his birthday licking mat with the look of a starving hound and finished it in two seconds flat. 😂
My gorgeous boy has taught me so much about myself and we're on a fantastic journey together filled with love, laughter and quite a large pinch of "what the flip?" for both of us. 😂💚💚💚
He is "Simply the Best"

Lots of love,
Carrie xxx

5th April 2020 Carrie into online dog training group

Time for a little serious sharing. We all have our struggles and it's sometimes good to hear we're not alone.

So, here goes ...
Oberon is a sweetheart, a bundle of joy and makes me laugh every single day but he is also a bucket load of stress. He is particularly vocal today!! But that's my fault. Walking him two days in a row with Othello is a mistake!! I knew that before I did it, but I needed to do it today. I love the little guy to bits, but his neediness is very, very, tiring. I reckon I get no more than an hour most days when he isn't stuck to me like velcro. This is work in progress!

I decided to look back at the issues I had noted down over the first week or two of having him.
1. Barking around food.
2. Extremely bad diarrhoea.
3. Separation Anxiety – whining, barking, howling.
4. Whining/squeaking constantly on walks.
5. Barking at anything/everything on walks.
6. Not toileting on walks.

Progress:
1. Not a problem after 24 hours once I upped his feeds.
2. It took 6 weeks to get a diagnosis, but it cleared up relatively quickly after that.
3. Probably no better, although there have been occasional glimmers of hope.
4. Very rarely happens now. Maybe once in every ten walks.
5. Mostly under control. He doesn't bark at dogs in gardens that are barking. On occasion, he does bark at another dog in the road if it barks first.
6. Happily toileting to his heart's content.

So, progress is being made.

The Separation Anxiety creates stress for everyone in the house, but particularly for me. It can make me feel like I'm failing and responsible for everyone being hacked off. I still get a bit tearful some days when I feel exhausted by it. Until we went into lockdown the only person who had to hear it was me, but of course everyone is home now and everyone is a dog

training expert 😂😂😂😂😂 If I listened to all their advice I would be never leaving him alone, at the same time as leaving him to cry himself into exhaustion, while systematically rewarding him for howling and shouting at him for howling to toughen him up. 😂😂

It's a good job I have broad shoulders (most days) a sense of humour (most days) and wine to look forward to (at weekends mostly 😉).

Everything is, of course, OK when I look into those loving and trusting eyes and he rests his head on my knee, just because he loves me.

Lots of love,
Carrie xxx

I got to play in mud and swim in the river.
It really is shaping up to be a great birthday.

LD is very noisy today. Carrie says it's because he still needs to relax after yesterday's walk.
I still think he just likes the sound of his own voice 😂😂
He's been super howly today and everyone is getting a bit fed up with him 😕

Carrie tried the treat machine in his pen today, but he was too upset to eat 😢
He is better if I'm with him but if both Carrie and I go away he has a complete meltdown.

Poor LD. He's a sad boy sometimes.
Carries's daughter, Jo, said that drugs might be the answer, but I'm not sure if that's for Carrie or LD 😂😂

Lots of love,
Othello xxx

6th April 2020

I woke up to find that the cats left a mouse in our box of noisy toys this morning 👍👍
I think they missed the point though as it wasn't squeaking any more 😂
I can think of other tastier things that they could have left to save me scouring the flower beds 😉

Had a nice little walk with just Carrie today.

Carrie says walking me helps to alleviate the stress of having Oberon 😂😂😂
Which is actually really funny as it used to be me that was stressing her on walks 😂😂😂
Of course, I'm a well-behaved boy now 😉

I have decided that in order to get more treats, I will pretend to not understand how to play some of the high energy games.
This means that Carrie keeps throwing out treats to reset me and I just keep acting dumb.
Ahh, the bliss of playing games and confusing Carrie.
It makes my life such fun 😂💚
I think I will apply my thinking to as many games as possible 😂😂

Yours, thoughtfully,
Othello xxx

I did play waiting for tweats.
I did be patient.
I did get treats.
I did bark at blender.

7th April 2020

Morning from Othello in a very sunny Wales.

I have been giving Carrie what looks like my adoring look, which always guarantees a couple of treats.
Between us, I'm actually wondering when she's going to pluck her eyebrows, as there's a danger she's letting things slip during lockdown 😏
I guess if she starts plaiting her under arm hair then everything is lost 😂😂

There are some big black bales of silage on our walk which weren't there yesterday, so I mulled over whether it was worth a bark or not and decided against it.
Good call on my part as I got a few more treats 😊
There were also lots of squashed frogs on the road but I know they taste nasty so I left them alone (I picked one up once when I was a wee pup and boy was it disgusting 😔)

Between you and me, I might have done a little shoulder-dip into some dry bird poo 😏😏 but let's keep that between ourselves or Carrie will do her over excited-dance!

Lots of love,

Your friend,
Othello xxx

I az been chewing mys chew.
Cawwie iz not yummy wike sniffing iz.
I did not bark at dog who was barking.

Dog did bark at I.
I does not like rose thorns 😕
Dey does prickle mys nose.

Wuv U

8th April 2020

I hope you are all staying safe and well during these very strange times.

As Carrie doesn't want to leave LD today because of his Separation Anxiety, we went on the treadmill.
I quite like it because there are always treats at the end, but LD has always been super scared of it.
I don't think I was ever scared of it, but I am a very brave boy.
Carrie has been giving him treats for just looking at it (spoilt brat 😂😂) and letting him watch us.
Today he put a paw on it which thrilled Carrie.
I can't really see what the fuss is about but hey-ho at least he wasn't howling 😀

Not going for a walk limits the quantity of delicious things I can find to eat so I will have to check out the flower beds later for prizes the cats may have left.

There is always a possibility that someone will leave the gate open to the duck pen too which is a triple whammy because there is duck food, duck poo and the delicious water they swim in to drink 😊

Love,
Othello xxx

Morning!
Did not bark at vacuum.
Did not bark at airdryer.
Did steal Cawwies trainer.
Did steal her sock.

Wuv U

9th April 2020

Good morning from Othello in sunny Wales.

It was super busy on my walk with Carrie.
I saw a black dog that I know on the other side of the road.
Once upon a time I would have pulled Carrie across the road to get to play with it, and probably barked, but now I just ignore it.
I think training Carrie to pay attention to me AND feed me yummy treats has really helped.
I also saw a lady with a dog, but they were of no interest to me either.
I was playing frisbee and Middle which is much more fun than they are 😏
I did sneak a bit of sheep poo but I think I deserved it and I also swam in some lovely water pools 😬

There were some interesting smells out there today, but I resisted them and we played games.

Last night there was a cat fight in the village, and I showed LD how to chant to support the winner.
I don't think Carrie was pleased with me though.

Lots of love,
From Othello xxx

Saw a frog.
Wanted frog.
Not allowed frog 😩
Did not bark.
Get frog next time.

Wuv U

10th April 2020

Morning from Othello!!

Another beautiful day in Wales.
Had a lovely walk and played lots of games on and around some big stones.

I was feeling angelic, so I didn't eat the horse poo that was right in the middle of the track and I ran back to Carrie even though I was trying to track a critter.
It was worth it though as there were extra yummy treats waiting for me.

The water in the river was just the right temperature for a swim.
Carrie only ran off once, and I was right behind her, so she only got a few steps away.
I'm finding the more I keep my eyes on her the less she does that now, so her training is coming along 😂

Your friend,
Othello xxx

11th April 2020

We're not going for a walk until later as Carrie has stuff to do.
I'm very good at chilling out so this suits me, and we get filled KONGS which we both love.
We have them separately 'cos LD tries to steal mine 😟

I think I'm going to have a walk this evening. I'll keep you updated if anything exciting happens.
Have a great day and I hope you laugh as much as Carrie does most days 😁😁😁

Lots of love,
Othello xxx

Saw people.
Did not bark.
Dogs barked at I.
I did not bark.
More dogs barked at I.
I did bark.
Like playing games.
Yesterday Jo sat wiv I while Cawwie walked Thello.
I did bark for a long time.
Jo had an eadache.

Wuv U

12th April 2020

LD and I have just been a-chilling, literally all day.
Carrie has been pottering around doing work, so we've just been practising being calm.
LD has been tremendous at it today, just sleeping on his bed.

We did look for the Easter Bunny this morning while the people all had their traditional Easter Egg hunt, but sadly it was long gone.

Hope you've all had a fabulous Easter.

Lots of love,
Othello xxx

** Update **
While we were walking this evening, Truffles and I let Carrie be more interesting than a deer drinking from the river!!

I suspect she will be extremely pleased with us for some time now 

Love from,
Othello The Angelic xxx

13th April 2020

I played a bit of putting my front paws on stuff today.
It's a great way of getting treats for not very much work.

LD is very keen to do a lot of work to get a few measly treats but I'm all about energy conservation.

There is always stuff on the news about it so I'm very modern in my thinking.
I also do my bit to cut down on food waste, as you all know, by keeping a close eye on the bins too.
I consider my efforts to tidy up after the cats a vital job as well, 'cos we all know how dangerous cat poo is.
So, in my own way I feel I am becoming more environmentally friendly by the day.

It's very important in these days of uncertainty to find a hobby that brings us joy.

Lots of love,
Othello xxx

Two Paws On iz easy wiv good treats.
Ard with bad treats.
Leg Weaves.
Same.
Barking.
Dont need treats.
I iz clever.

Wuv U

14th April 2020

A very exciting morning out there today!

Carrie DMT'd me as we walked past some horses and I was concentrating so hard that I slipped off the kerb.
I limped a bit to lay on the guilt and got lots of sympathy and treats 😊

We went on a bit further and some huge dogs were doing their pieces at the fence and sassing it up like never before.
Well, I like playing hard to get so I just ignored them completely and let Carrie drip feed me some treats.
Clearly, they think I am very alluring 😂😂

We were playing some more games in the forest when all of a sudden there was a man with a huge camera coming towards us!
I gave him my most impressive bark but stopped when Carrie told me not to.
I then sat watching her while she chatted to him about badgers and deer.
Yawn … they went on for ages and I did do a couple of little whines 'cos they seemed to have forgotten me.
We had just heard the first cuckoo for this year. He said he was trying to find it so he could take some photos.
Strange that he didn't want photos of me!
Eventually, we set off again and played ball 😀😀😀 for a while.

On the way home Carrie decided to "risk forward" whatever that means? So, I walked back past the huge dogs off my lead and got liver treats! 😀

I love a lamb, mainly because they are so damn cute.
People sometimes bring sick ones for Carrie to help, so I've met lots of them.
I find them hard to resist but I did resist the ones in the field today so more treats came my way 😂😂

I'm off for a nap now.
Stay safe everyone.

Lots of love,
Othello xxx

Played Toy Switch.
I wike Toy Switch.
Can get two toys in mys mouth at once 😄

Did not bark.
Cawwie says liver treats are my Achilles eel.

Wuv U

15th April 2020

I've only had a little walk today as I have a hurty leg.
I think I did it when I slipped off the kerb.
Carrie says I have to rest it for a little while.
Take care everyone.

Lots of love,
Othello xxx

Saw sheep.
Not bark.
Eard army guns.
Not bark.
Saw lady with dogs.
Not bark.
Lady said I iz gwowing into a good puppy.
I iz pleased.

Wuv U

16th April 2020

I am feeling a bit left out as I've not had a walk today and LD came back with tales of barking sheep, huge black horses, and sassy dogs.
The way he tells it you would think he'd been fighting off dragons 😂

I've had a nice chew but it really didn't last very long, so I was a bit disappointed in it.
I know there are some stuffed KONGS in the freezer so I'm hoping one comes my way soon.

Carrie has been trying to teach me to touch her hand with my nose, but I can't see much fun in that, so I'm acting dumb.
I do know what she wants as LD does it, but I'm working those treats. 😏
I know how to touch the target on the treat dispenser. I think that's plenty of touching.

After all, her hands just smell way too clean these days 😂
Everyone is constantly washing their hands because of the virus.
Of course, mugging Carrie's pockets for treats is different because that's not touching hands.
I like to cosy up to her on the sofa and have a quick rummage.

One of the teenagers is outside painting the gate so I have high hopes that I can get some paint on LD's fur later 😂😂

Lots of love,
Othello xxx

Saw a horse.
I did not bark.
Saw a lady.
I did not bark.
Sheep barked at I.

I did not bark.
Sassy hounds barked.
I did not bark.
Cawwie is wewy appy.
I got treats.
I iZ appy 😁

Wuv U

17th April 2020

Not much to report today but I went for a little walk this morning and really wanted to play ball.
Carrie said not to, in case my leg hurt again 🙁

I did get that yummy stuffed KONG yesterday, which helped a lot with my boredom.
I've been playing gentle games at home.

I've been asking for, and getting, lots of cuddles, I'm hoping to get out into the garden later to tidy up after the cats.

Sadly, I failed to get paint on LD yesterday as it dried very quickly.
The teenagers got covered in it which makes no sense to me as they said they weren't trying to 😏 so I think they might have had a fight with it.
Lots of love,

From Othello xxx

I ave been practising Down.
I fink itZ silly.
I owled when Cawwie walked Thello.
Some dogs barked at I wen I waZ outside.

I did not bark.
Dogs barked again.
I did bark.

Wuv U

18th April 2020

Morning!

My leg is feeling much better today so we might play frisbee again next week.

For some reason the sheep were very sassy today and came right up to the fence to stare.
It might be because they have lambs.
I have to be honest and say I did think about doing a little bark and pull towards one.
I remembered immediately that I don't do that anymore, so I spun straight back around and looked at Carrie to get a nice treat.
Carrie said it was a momentary lapse and that we all get those sometimes 😂😂

There were some horses in a field earlier.
I don't mind them unless they pop their heads up over the hedge and then I jump.
Bet they'd jump too if I did it to them 😂 of course I wouldn't though as I am very polite 😉😂

Found a couple of yummy treats under the raised bed earlier and I surprised myself at how flat I can make myself if I need to 😉
Apparently, I looked very inelegant with my bum pointing out, but Carrie was lucky I didn't parp 😂😂
Have a great weekend.

Lots of love,
Othello xxx

Oberon here.
I weally wike playing games.

Wuv U

<u>19th April 2020</u>

It was nice to get out for a walk today as LD woke up with a lot of bounce in him which quickly resulted in whining 😟

There are men harvesting trees in the forest. This meant it was worth a scout around for left over lunches, but my hunt was futile.
Carrie was generous with liver treats, so I kept pretty close to her.
I tried a few darts off into the woods, but the Knicker Elastic didn't need to stretch far today 😂😂😂

I'm pleased to say that en route to the car I managed to do a bit of tidying up after the cats before Carrie noticed and put her stern voice on.

The cats have picked somewhere new to leave presents which makes the garden a very exciting place 😏
They also left entrails on the conservatory floor this morning, but if they aren't going to eat it there's no way I want it!

We thought I was all better, but my leg isn't quite right yet and it hurt when I jumped into the car after our walk.
Carrie says no more car journeys for a while.

We don't very often go in the car so that's OK with me.
Have a good day everyone.

Lots of love,
Othello xxx

I ave cided to be noisy today coz I can.
Played some fun games wiv Cawwie.
Did bark sometimes.
Fink I might be annoying everyone 😉

Wuv U

20th April 2020

Cawwie took I to the field and I did running.
She kept running in diffrent directions.
Every time I ran past her she ran somewhere else.
It waz fun but puffy.

Wuv U

21st April 2020

Morning from Othello in sunny Wales.

I was allowed a walk today, but no frisbee ☹

I did ignore two cock pheasants fighting which got me some nice treats, and then more when they flew off.
There are lots of birds fighting at the moment and they dance about on the tracks right in front of my snozzle, tempting me to be naughty 😂😂
DMT'd away from a cross sheep with her lamb and then had a nice time swimming in a water pool in the sun.
Played a few gentle games and then came home to find everyone complaining about LD's barking and howling!

Sloppy kisses,
Othello xxx

I ad a bath and I waz wewy good.
I did not bark at de airdryer.

Wuv U

22nd April 2020

Morning from Othello

Firstly, I would like all my dog friends to know that cat food is definitely nicer than dog food.
I will say no more on the subject though, as Carrie has strong opinions about me eating it 😔

We had a lovely walk and I was allowed a few ball chases, but not many as I still have to take care of my leg.

We walked past a dog in its garden and it came to the fence to shout at me, but I was focused on Carrie, so I just ignored him.
The sassy dogs were up at the fence barking, and on the other side were sheep with lambs, but I gobbled up treats and all was well.
We then gently played a few games, which was just lovely in the sun.

Carrie was hoping to take a public path through a field on the way back, but we couldn't, so we had to pass the sheep and sassy dogs again.
I know Carrie was wondering how it would turn out, as she thought I might have used up all my good for the day 😂😂
One of the lambs was right up at the fence staring at me and the hounds were running the fence on the other side.
Even though I was trying hard not to, I did do a little pull towards the lamb and then corrected myself.
Carrie said it was a tough situation though and I had done my very best 😀
Have a lovely day everyone.

Lots of love,
Othello xxx

22nd April 2020

I ave been doing agility.
I wike cheese better dan jumping though 😄😄
I waz not going on de seesaw but I did wike de tunnel.

Wuv U

24th April 2020

Carrie said it was time for some fun, so we had a lovely walk and swim with no rules.
LD is so brave now and jumped into the river with us.
I think he looks like a beaver when he swims 😂😂
Apparently, we were all well behaved (even the teenage boys!) 😂
There was lots of fun and laughter with treats for us dogs.

Your friend,
Othello xxx

I ad to scramble onto Cawwie to get a share of de cuddles cos everybodys wanted dem.
I waz wewy wet😁😁😁

Wuv U

25th April 2020

What a lovely time we had again in the river.
I swam with Truffles and LD for ages and even Tofu came in for a paddle.
We only played quiet games as it's really hot today.

Love,
Othello xxx

26th April 2020

One of the boy teenagers has got a new basketball hoop so I'm keen to help him fetch the ball but I'm not allowed.
Something about not wanting me to put holes in it???
It's tough when your past indiscretions are held against you 😟
Carrie says it's good for me to work on my impulse-control but clearly has no idea how much work I put in already … not eating cat food, not rummaging bins, not chasing the cats.
I could go on but I'm sure you get the idea.
Have a lovely day.

Lots of love from,
Othello xxx

27th April 2020

So, this morning may not have been the best representation of my behaviour 😂😂
I got bored while Carrie was talking to someone over the gate. The woman was very excitable and the more excited she became the louder and more squeaky she got.
I'm afraid I gave her a bark … oops, it just slipped out 😏
On the plus side, Carrie then said her goodbyes and we went for a walk.
We had just got under way when a flipping ginger cat danced across the road in front of us and (you guessed it) I did a little bark at him.
To be honest, I do know better.
Carrie DMT'd until we passed by the cat's house and I did then behave impeccably.
Frankly, if Carrie had been paying better attention then I could have been scoffing treats instead of barking, so it's really her fault 😂😂😂
When we got to the forest we played some games and I ignored the six dogs who came rushing towards me and I got loads of treats.

Big licks,
Othello xxx

Cawwie az been trying to play games wiv I and I iz more interested in scratching iself and rolling around.
So now I ave to lie on mys boundary and be calm ... sigh

Wuv U

28th April 2020

Morning!

I am dizzy because of the speed I have been moving at while playing games ... just like a cartoon character!

I was pleased with myself for catching a few treats while we were playing, and also for my ability to squeeze under chairs to pick up the ones that Carrie dropped so badly 😂😂

For some reason Carrie could not make up her mind if I was to sit or lie down, so I was bouncing up and down like a rabbit on a sugar rush 😂😂 (disclaimer ... of course I would not condone a rabbit being given sugar or any other testing on animals).
Have a good day and enjoy the rain if you're in Wales.

Lots of love,
Othello xxx

29th April 2020

Carrie and I managed to get out for our walk before the rain came.

It was exciting this morning!!

I was wandering around off the lead with Truffles when all of a sudden, a load of sheep starting running on the other side of a hillock.
The fence had come down and Carrie hadn't noticed (away with the fairies again 😂).
Truffles, being a collie, started to run towards them, and I followed her.
Carrie called at us to come back and we both spun around and charged back to her.
Boy, did we get lots of treats 😀😀😀😀😊😊
I felt pretty pleased with myself as I weighed it all up and thought "Middle and treats" is better than sheep.
Truffles was all like "there's always another sheep, let's get those treats".
She's older and wiser than me though 😉

Love,
Othello xxx

30th April 2020

Fortunately, Carrie has not been inclined to drag me out in the rain so I'm snoozing on the sofa after a few games.

I'm awfully glad I don't have fluffy fur like LD 'cos he is always being titivated. Carrie's been combing him again today.

I have found zero mischief today so I'm feeling rather angelic 😇
Stay dry everyone.

Sloppy kisses,
Othello xxx

Chapter Eight
'Cows and Kapows'

2nd May 2020

I'm staring out of the window wondering if I am ever going out for a walk.

I don't usually mind staying at home when it's raining but today I feel like I'm missing out.

Apart from a few games in the house, I've done nothing today … sigh.

To make the most of the situation, I will use this time to make a mind map of future fun.

LD went out for a walk, and then Carrie has been in and out of the house doing "stuff" in the garden.

The cats left entrails on the path again but even I wouldn't touch those. I'm not that bored! 😉

Hope you are all having more excitement than me.

Lots of love,
Othello xxx

2nd May 2020

Dog barked.
I did not bark.
Annuver dog gwowled.
I did not gwowl.
I did play in mud 😆

Wuv U

3rd May 2020

Morning!

Today, I am wearing my ears in a slightly more stylish fashion 😂
They are folded inside out.

Had a very nice scatter feed in the garden and a licking mat with yummy stuff on.
All before LD got up this morning.
I like that time of day because it's just me and Carrie having a chill time.
When LD gets up he is crazy with excitement 😂

I had an on the lead walk yesterday evening which was very pleasant as the sun was out.
The sun did an excellent job of warming up the sheep poo that was squashed into the road, making the bits I managed to snaffle very tasty indeed.

When we got home, I rounded it off with a few mouthfuls of grass which had a definite spring bouquet about them 😜

Using my mind map, I did a quick hunt in the flower beds but it proved fruitless.

It wasn't a complete waste of time though as I did some pretty sharp recalls to earn a few treats and cuddles.

Sniffs and licks,
Othello xxx

Played touch, spin and Kapow in de garden today.
Kapow is gweat cos Cawwie just shouts it an I getz to run after er.
Appawently Mr Knotty has been in my fur and I ave to be brushed again.
I managed to scuttle de cat earlier, but I didnt get any treats 😕

Wuv U

4th May 2020

LD and I had a very nice walk together.
Truffles and Jo came too.
There was a silly sheep out on the road with her lambs, but we really weren't bothered by her and she ran off trailing her lambs behind her.

The interesting thing about running sheep is that they leave lots of little treats behind them.
I think you can imagine how happy we were with our little snacks 😋😋
I think Carrie said something about "picking her battles" 😂

We were allowed to go off the lead as the road was so quiet, and we played a game where we all go sniffing and then Carrie calls us back.

First back gets the tastiest treat.
Sadly for me, Truffles is very fast 😵 but even second and third best treats are very yummy 😀
Have a lovely rest of your day everyone.

Lots of love,
Othello xxx

5th May 2020

We had a lovely walk this morning.
Lots of running when Carrie shouted Kapow.
She did it several times, so I think she is going through one of her forgetful phases.
Thank goodness she remembered the treats 😂

Saw some big black cows and then a dog that appeared from nowhere.
The cows were of no interest to me, but the dog was pretty exciting, so it took us a couple of calls before we ran back to Carrie.
He was a very barky and bouncy dog, so it was tempting to have a play.
However, good sense prevailed along with tasty treats 😂😂

It was necessary to have a wee dip in the mucky water pools today as we weren't close enough to the river.
It is vital to "take the waters" every day to keep us healthy.

LD is about to have yet another bath 😂😂

Sloppy kisses,
Othello xxx

I did see cows.
I did bark at cows.
Did play in de mucky water.
Did get ANNUVER bath ... sigh.

Wuv U

6th May 2020

We had a lovely walk earlier.

I think it's best to start with the positives:
1. The sun was shining.
2. We both ran straight back to Carrie instead of investigating the man who was planting trees in the forest.
3. The bird poo I found to roll in was almost dried up, which meant not much of it stuck to my fur.
4. The puddle that Oberon played in was only 90% mud.
5. I think we both smell lovely.
The negatives:
1. Carrie did not seem to see the poo incident in the same light as me and did her excited dance 😂😂😂
2. Carrie said I stink.
3. I will be hosed down.
4. LD will probably get another bath

Your long suffering friend,
Othello xxx

7th May 2020

I would like to report that there were no mud incidents this morning, but I can't 😂😂😂😂

Of course, I only went in water
LD played in mud until he was just thick with it.
He cracks me up 😂😂😂
He covered Carrie in it too because he ran to her to give her muddy hugs

We played Kapow a few times for yummy fish treats.
Other than that we were just free spirits.
There was literally nothing out in the forest today, so it was a very quiet walk.

No prizes for guessing what is going to happen to LD later 😂😂😂😂

Lots of love,
Othello xxx

I saw mud.
I got into de mud.
Waz wuverly.

9th May 2020 Carrie into online dog training group

A whole year has gone by since my gorgeous chocolate Labrador left to play in the field of dreams.
Still miss him so much.

I thought I would share the poem I wrote for him at the time.

A tribute to my beautiful doggy friend, Thornton.

I wake up in the morning
And for second I forget
You're not there by my side
Your touch, your smell, your breath
You made my life a joy to live
Your love, your heart, your soul
You knew me like no other did
And now my life's not whole
I hope you knew my love for you
Was deeper than the ocean
I know you felt my highs and lows
My every last emotion
You were a hero for the kids
Our friend, a cherished ear
A beacon of true love and warmth
Someone to keep near
For all the days we had together
For being my best friend
I'll hold you in my heart, my dear
Until the very end.

We went on a walk that Thornton loved today.
It included a swim in his favourite part of the river and even the terriers went in.
He and I used to stand by the river together waiting for permission to jump in.
He was the one who gave me the courage to take my very first dip 🩶

Carrie, Jo and The Youngest Boy took a picnic but they were not willing to share, so we just kept shaking close to them so they had soggy sandwiches 😂😂😂
While the four of us were employed doing that, Truffles had great fun taking big stones out of the river.

She collected them into a pile and then put them in the river somewhere else.
No idea why, but she was happy 😀
We played a lot of running back into Middle and we are all currently napping.

Love from,
Othello xxx

10th May 2020

Morning!

Apparently, a huge stretch of muddy water is not suitable for us to swim in!! Crazy eh???

I did get a huge compliment from Carrie after I found another lovely pool to swim in though 😀
She said I smell like a badger's bum ... brilliant or what? 😂😂
I thought about asking how she knew but then decided I didn't need to know 😏😏

LD found a new game earlier, which is rolling in bracken until he comes out looking like he's wearing camouflage 😂😂

It's about to rain so we're having a nap.

Lots of love,
Othello xxx

I did roll in bracken.
I did wike it.
Thello smellz.

Wuv U

11th May 2020

It feels very cold here today, but we managed to find some sun while we were out.
I took a stick home to put on the wood burner as I think we might have to light it later.
I'm very helpful like that 😂😂

We've both been banned from swimming for a while as I've "broken" my tail from over exertion in the cold water.
It will be fine again soon as it usually just takes a few days to be back in full wag mode.

I have been cheered up immensely by the lovely package that our special friend Barnaby Brown sent us.
Barnaby is a very generous and handsome chap and he's always very sympathetic about my struggles with Carrie 😉
The package smells divine and is full of yummy dog chews.
Carrie has put it up very high, so we don't "disgrace ourselves" 😂😂
I've no idea what she thinks we might do? 😜

Unless it's linked to the bit of an accident I had earlier.

I accidentally took the lid off the treat tin and had a little sample, then I heard someone coming and gobbled some down so quickly that I couldn't breathe 😏
Carrie said she had no sympathy for me which I think is rather mean of her 😟

We played some Knicker Elastic and Kapow on our walk.
LD is now such a fast runner that he always gets back first.

Sloppy kisses,
Othello xxx

We played games.
We got treats.
I iz faster dan Thello!
A box wiv nice smellZ arrived in de post.
I cant find it now.
I fink Cawwie must ave hid it.
Cant fink why ☹
Thello sed it did cum from Barnabee Bwown.
E iz wuverly and iz mys an Thellos fweind.

Wuv U 

12th May 2020

I ave a new Blackdog ead collar.
We've been playing Cone game practising getting I ready to wear it for agez.
Saw horses and dogs.
I did not bark.

Wuv U 

13th May 2020

It's still chilly where we are, but we had a nice walk.
Apparently, two hares ran across the track in front on us, but we were watching Carrie so closely that we missed them!!
I wish they had bells on like the chocolate Easter rabbits, then I would know they are about.
At least then I could choose whether to chase or not 😉

I've been doing extra training with Carrie early in the morning before LD gets up, as she just concentrates better then 😂😂
I'm enjoying that time very much as it's our alone time (plus I get all the fuss and treats) 😊
We don't get much time alone as LD is coming on walks with us at the moment because he's getting stressed at home.

Love,
Othello xxx

14th May 2020 Carrie into online dog training group after recent consult with Dr Tom Mitchell, Behavet

I'm feeling a little emotional now (understatement 😄😄). For the first time in literally months I've had a shower while leaving Oberon in his pen, and there was not a peep out of him. He didn't even have Othello in the room with him.
I've followed Tom's instructions to the letter since Oberon's behaviour consultation last week, and it's already paying off!!!
Tom knows his stuff and really made me feel like there was a route forward for us.

Lots of love,
Carrie xxx

I am happy to report that I had some unexpected "Terry Time" yesterday and he is still more alluring than anything else (including Carrie) 😂
We bumped into him in the forest on our walk so I just started trotting at his heels gazing lovingly up at him 😊

I do not understand LD he just isn't interested in him at all, and oddly that makes Carrie seem happy ... weird ehh??

Carrie said we weren't allowed to play sticks or any other kind of fetch because of my recent injuries, but that was OK because I saw my bestie.
Every time Carrie called me back to Middle I ran to Terry 'cos sometimes he accidentally drops treats 😏
I love that dude 😀😀

Yours, happily,
Othello xxx

Terry who??

15th May 2020

Shh ... I might be a tiny bit guilty 😂😂

I have just finished off LD's scatter feed while Carrie was outside with him ... whoops!!
I even managed to crawl under his raised bed to get a few lost ones that were there.
Carrie said that considering how I struggle to go under her legs when we're playing, she finds it difficult to comprehend.
Clearly, she doesn't realise that the highest value treat is a stolen one 😉
She doesn't really mind though as he didn't want it anyway.

Carrie hid my kibble in some rolled up blankets today, so I had to rummage really hard to get it.

Sniffs and licks,
Othello xxx

15th May 2020 Carrie into online dog training group.

Had an epic fail this morning!! I should have trusted my gut and not left Oberon while I went for my shower. He barked and howled the whole time. It wasn't a failing on his part, but a failing on mine for pushing the little guy too fast.
Lesson learnt.

Lots of love,
Carrie xxx

16th May 2020

It was cold last night and there were lots of stars out!!

How does he know this you might be asking yourself?
Because I got Carrie up twice in the night to admire the sky while I produced a few squishy presents for her 😊

I was a little worried that breakfast might not be on the menu today, but she came through with a few food games which was a relief as my tummy was a-rumbling 😬😬

LD woke up howling this morning, we could hear him from in the garden where we were playing frisbee.

Hugs,
Othello xxx

I woked up an owled.

17th May 2020

I am exhausted.

Just had a walk with three puppies and, boy, were they a handful!!
I was hoping to get some "Terry Time" but sadly I just got time with his pup, Dougal, Bella and another pup while he went off cycling.

Being the generous spirit that I am, I introduced them to the joys of sheep droppings. I know they will thank me for forever 😂😂
Carrie didn't appreciate my teachings and put me back on the lead 😟

Both LD and I set very good examples with our recalls though and got lots of treats.

Love,
Othello xxx

18th May 2020

I had to go in the river after rolling in bird poo.
Carrie was busy filming LD rolling down the bank and totally missed what I was doing 😂😂😂
LD came in too, but he was so dirty that he still needed a bath.
Let's be honest, no amount of Carrie's treats are even nearly as good as a squidgy bird poo 😊
The Youngest Boy threw sticks into to river for me to try and get the smell out of my fur.
It was great fun and made me go a bit deaf 😉

Doggy love,
Othello xxx

Oberon here.
I did some rolling.
I ad a bath.

19th May 2020

Just had 10 minutes one-to-one with Carrie, which was an unexpected bonus off the back of LD being a bit of a monkey.
He was in the pen with Carrie in the room and she gave him a very delicious treat.
She thought he hadn't noticed it so she went to point it out and he barked and grabbed it quickly.

Anyway, she decided that she needed some time out so we went outside and played Middle, Two Paws On and Toy Switch.

Poric reported that LD started howling and barking four minutes after we left.

Carrie is not having the best day because she stepped in mouse entrails first thing 😂
I'd already seen them and decided they weren't of any interest, so I left them in situ.

Lots of love,
Othello xxx

I ad a walk wiv Piper.
I humped Piper.
Piper growled at I.
Cawwie said it waz mys own fault!
We played some fun games.

Wuv U

20th May 2020 into online dog training group

Othello and Oberon just recalled from a sheep and her two lambs that appeared from nowhere right in front of them! They were both super surprised and when the sheep took off at full speed the boys thought about chasing, but turned straight back when I called them.
Very proud of them both 💕💕💕💕🎉🎉

Lots of love,
Carrie xxx

It's a crazy world at the moment!!

We were having a nice walk in the sun this morning when we came across a holly bush with berries on it!!
I thought it was winter again for a minute!
Carrie gave me a treat and I dropped sheep poo that was already in my mouth ... that, my friends, was a tough call I can tell you 😀
We also both recalled from a very interesting smell which we felt was worth investigating.
We were half-way up a grass bank before Carrie noticed, hot on its trail and it was probably going to be a real humdinger of a treat ...
I suspect it was a 7-10 day vintage 😂😂

LD woke up this morning and started howling, even though Carrie had got up early to try to get one step ahead of him 😂😂
He's a little 🐵

He found a dead mouse in the garden last night, but he didn't eat it or run off with it. Boring!!

We are hoping for a dip in the paddling pool later to cool us off.

Big kisses,
Othello xxx

I did owl.
I do not wike kibble.
So der.

Wuv U

21st May 2020

Morning!

I think some of you have heard about our epic win with Carrie yesterday evening.
We were minding our own beeswax when a sheep with her lambs suddenly appeared … now in the past that would have sent Carrie into a frenzy and we might have found the thought of chasing those sheep very tempting.
But all those hours of training finally paid off. She called us and when we got to her we had high value treats, none of that rubbish kibble that she used to palm us off with 😂
She remained calm (you know how long we've been working on calmness 😏) and her voice wasn't squeaky.
The bonus was that she remembered to trust us and just walk the other way without sticking us on the lead!
I think I have mastered the DMT (Don't Make Trouble) behaviour now 😏
Over all, we are very proud of her.

This morning I decided to invest in being "alert" as I've heard that's what they are doing in England, because of the virus, and the tactic may come to Wales.
So, in a very alert way I pounced into the long grass after a mouse and then used my alert behaviour to run back to Carrie for treats 😀

I alertly followed a sniffy trail for a few seconds and then with growing alertness rushed back to Carrie.

I did have a bit of a grassy bum incident earlier as I over-indulged yesterday 😂😂
Things were a bit tricky for a few minutes as I could see that Carrie was gagging a bit when she thought she might be required to help out 😏
It all ended well though 😀

Incidentally, the pool was a blast yesterday afternoon.

Take care.

Love from,
Othello xxx

I did owl dis morning.
I did roll in grass cuttings.
I did wike de paddling pool.

Wuv U

22nd May 2020

I, once again, started the day by helping Carrie with her workout.
I find licking her ear always spurs her on to work harder.

I had breakfast in the box of toys this morning and BOY did I rattle and jangle its contents around.
Luckily, I didn't wake LD, so I got a bit of time alone with Carrie 😀

There were bits of left-over bird in the conservatory this morning but sadly Carrie didn't step in them so there was no crazy dance from her.
If I'm in the mood, I love to see her dance, and other times I hide my face with embarrassment.

I continue to practise "being alert" and have so far noticed the removal of the treat tin lid and the piece of popcorn down the side of the fridge.
Also, being alert has gained me extra treats for becoming intrigued by a blackbird hopping on the track. They are everywhere and you never know which one to be alert to! 😉

Both of us went into super-alert mode when we were out walking because when we looked back, Carrie wasn't there!
We ran like demons fearing the worst and wondering if this thing that we should be alert to had got her!
However, all was well, she'd just wandered off the track and was hiding behind a tree.
Carrie suggests that the thing we need to be alert to may be a Humphrey as you never know when to watch out for one as they are always about (she also thinks most of you are too young to understand that 😂😂😂)

Lots of love,
Othello xxx

22nd May 2020 Carrie into the online dog training group

Almost reaching the end of another week and I've resisted the temptation to climb out of the bathroom window and run away from LD yet again. 😂😂
Huge points to me!!
How many times has this boy reduced me to tears this week? Three (totally due to his anxiety about needing to be stuck to me like velcro).
How many times has he made me laugh or smile? Countless!
How many times has he recalled on a walk? Every one (occasionally after

thinking for a second but he still did it). Plus, an excellent recall from loose sheep! 😀
How many times has he refused his kibble? Pretty much every time … but he'll eat Othello's. 😂
How many times has he got covered in mud on a walk? Every time he's been near mud. 😂
The bonus is he no longer barks at the hairdryer and enjoys a bath.
How many times has he resource guarded? Twice.
How many more puppies will I get? Zero. 😂😂 He's my 13th and he's beaten the desire out of me. 😂😂
How much wine will I drink this weekend? I couldn't possibly say as using alcohol as a crutch is clearly inappropriate behaviour 😂😀 My alter ego would suggest about a bottle and a half though. 😂😂😂

Lots of love,
Carrie xxx

23rd May 2020

Another interesting start to the day!

We stepped into the conservatory first thing to find that the cats had jumped on board with the "being alert" theme and had clearly been on duty all night.
It looked like they had sacrificed every mouse for miles around to the Egyptian Goddess Bastet.
Carrie made a pyre in the wood burner and said a few words of apology to them.

I imagine there must have been some additional sacrifice somewhere dedicated to the Rain God too as it's been hammering it down 😂😂😂

I had banana on my licking mat this morning which was probably a very pleasant taste.

I say probably but as you know I'm a Labrador and we don't actually taste much before it disappears 😄
I had the rest of my breakfast on a Ruffle Snuffle mat.

The gusting wind makes us both a bit crazy so we're not going for a walk yet.

Lots of love,
Othello xxx

A dog barked at I.
Did not bark back.
I did not bark a de boy on his bike.
The dog barked at I on de way home.
I did not bark back.
I did eat sheep poo.

Wuv U

24th May 2020

Afternoon from Othello.

We had a stunning "no rules" walk with a lovely play in a shady stream to cool down.

LD was more interested in chewing bark than posing for the camera.

He's going to get a bark in one way or another 😄😂

Lots of love from sunny Wales,
Othello xxx

I ave been brushed and sprayed with stuff to get knots out.
Now I needz mud.

Wuv U

25th May 2020

We had another nice walk in the sun today.

Carrie remembered her training and DMT'd all five of us from a passing cyclist. She really only has to call one of us back, as we do then all go tearing back to her for treats 😂😂
There was a little dip in the river for those of us who were feeling the heat.

I really wanted to stay with The Youngest Boy because he kept cycling ahead and coming back but I wasn't allowed because he throws stones for me 😞😞
Carrie says they will chip my lovely teeth 😟

We all played some recall games but nothing too fast as it was so hot.

I had to spit out sheep poo when Carrie noticed what I was doing 😉
Piper ate sheep poo nearly as big as his head 😂😂

Snuffles and licks,
Othello xxx

I found a tiny muddy puddle so I played in it.
I did bark at Tofu.

I did jump on Tofu.
He did growl at I.
Cawwie sez I ave to be calm all day now.

Wuv U

26th May 2020

We DMT'd from a distant dog that was walking towards us.
I was off my lead and I stayed close, but LD had to stay on his lead for a few minutes until he became calm enough to be free.
As I was so good, we played a bit of ball, but LD ran off with my ball and wouldn't give it back 😞 Carrie says I can have a game by myself later.

LD used to be frightened of the bags with little trees in which are left for planting in the forest, but he sticks his head right in now and looks really funny.

I was a little bit naughty because I jumped into an extremely muddy pond even though I was supposed to be focused on Carrie.
I really couldn't help myself, I was very hot 😂😂
Up until the last second she really thought I wasn't going to, but I did a sneaky little dash behind her legs and I was wallowing before she got a word out 😂😂
She said that I had surpassed myself earlier, so I could be forgiven – even though apparently I was very smelly 😂 I think stagnant water smells almost as good as bird poo but she has a funny nose 😉

Have a lovely day everyone.

Lots of love,
Othello xxx

27th May 2020

While we were walking this morning I got ten minutes of "me time" with Carrie. Jo put Oberon on his lead and took him and Truffles off in another direction while we played ball.
It was lovely 😀
We were working on impulse-control. I had to wait in Middle until Carrie let me fetch the ball. I was very good at it. After we played that I got some free time playing fetch 😀

Then we met back up and had a swim in the river.

We recalled from something that we heard in the bushes. Sadly, I don't know what it was.
I'm betting that it was something a lesser dog would have run away from though, like a lion 😉 or a bear.

Doggy Snuggles,
Othello xxx

28th May 2020 Carrie into the online dog training group

I'm working on Oberon getting less distracted when we're out and about. His job was to stay on a log while my son cycled by. He coped really well and only on the third occasion did he get down and look. That was my fault really as once or twice was good enough.
My son also cycled towards and away from us while we were walking on the track, passing by quite close, and Oberon was able to stay focused on me. He also came back from a dog that was running free, which was very hard for him as they'd been playing.
I'm very pleased with him.

Lots of love,
Carrie xxx

Oberon here.
Cawwie said I iz a good boy for coming away from a dog an ignoring de boy.

Wuv U

29th May 2020 Carrie into online training group

The Oberon Stretch Gauge

Week 2

Running away feelings: Zero.
Reduced to tears: Zero.
Laughs: Countless.
Recall: 90% (he's reaching that age 😆😆). He always comes back but he sometimes does it in a more leisurely fashion. However, once again he recalled from loose sheep. He disengaged from other dogs off their leads and also cyclists (including my son).
Kibble: I am mixing his kibble with some of Othello's, and wet food.
Mud: Only a few mud incidents, but purely because there is less around. 😉
Resource guarding: Zero, but perhaps I am just more vigilant.
How many more puppies will I get: Still Zero. 
How much wine will I drink this weekend? My alter ego says "about a bottle". 😆
Othello remains the keeper of (most of) my heart and (most of) my sanity. 💜
He is by no means perfectly behaved but he is a Super Star. 

Lots of love,
Carrie xxx

30th May 2020

While we were training I stopped for a little rummage around in some dandelions.
I was certain there was something in there worth snaffling down, but I got called away before a full investigation took place.
Don't fret though I have that place marked in my memory for later.

We didn't take LD. I'm pleased to say we left him at home with The Youngest Boy for about 15 minutes. Progress or what???
Don't get me wrong he's a cool little buddy but Carrie and I like a bit of "us time".
Carrie said that getting out of the house without him noticing was like a military operation involving a lot of smoke and mirrors, but we did it!!
Apparently, he did whine a bit but didn't bark or howl 😀

We had a training session where I just had to keep my focus on Carrie (ignore the dandelion incident 😂😂😂) and keep running back to her for treats.
What's not to like?
I think Carrie thinks the dandelion action was just me staying alert as per Government guidelines.
She has forgotten that it doesn't apply to Wales so please don't remind her as I foresee a lot of beneficial mileage in it for me 😏😏

Anyway, bye for now.
Have a lovely weekend.

Lots of love,
Othello xxx

Summer
20nd Jun – 21st Sept
2020

Chapter Nine
'"Terry Time" and a Tribal Rhyme'

1st June 2020

Today has been exciting already!

Some dogs threw themselves at the fence barking and snarling, but I just ignored them as they looked foolish.
Carrie says if you can't say anything nice it's best to say nothing at all so that's why I didn't say anything back to them. I did think some stuff though 😂😂

However, I did bark at a cat that was lurking in the hedge because it just sat and stared at me.

Carrie had to say "niiice" to me three times before I remembered that I wasn't supposed to bark ☹

We played a few games in the garden when we got home as Carrie said I was lacking focus.
Flipping Cheek!!!
Lol! There is nothing wrong with my focus, I can turn on a sixpence when she gets the ball out!!
Have a great day.

Love from,
Othello xxx

I ave been in de river wiv Truffles.
I barked and owled wen Carrie took Thello into de garden.
I does not wike being by iself 

Wuv U 

<u>2nd June 2020</u>

I've had a chew and I'm now chilling on my cool mat (see what I did there?).

I haven't had a walk yet as LD is being a baby 😟

However, I have a sneaky suspicion that there might be some "Terry Time" this evening as I heard Carrie talking on the phone!!! 😀😀😀😀😀
Shhh … I will update tomorrow.
Safe to say that if it happens Carrie will not feature on my horizon.
Good job that LD isn't smitten with him or she would feel completely redundant 😂😂
I think Terry likes me much better than LD. He says LD has stopped Carrie from having a normal life, but I can't think why 😂😂😂😂😂

Carrie and I did some training before LD got up this morning.

Lots of love,
Othello xxx

**** Edit**
Terry's car has broken down 😟 but Carrie is going to take us to the woods instead.

I played a wickle bit of Kapow and chasing after Cawwie.
I saw dogs.
I did not bark at dogs.
Enuff sed.

Wuv U

<u>3rd June 2020</u>

I have convinced Oberon to hold out for fish or liver treats if Carrie wants to feel more alluring than the environment 😊

**We went out yesterday evening before the rain started.
It was heaving out in the forest with cyclists and walkers popping up from nowhere.
Of course, by heaving I mean we saw a couple, but it feels a bit cheeky of them to be out during our fun time 😒
We were both excellent at recalling from the cyclists, but LD did run up to a walker. I stayed with Carrie and Jo and he soon came back to see why we weren't joining in the fun.**

We spotted many hares about too. They look like great fun to chase but we didn't as Carrie's treat bag kept rattling.

**We both had to go on our leads as we passed the muddy pond, something about not wanting a repeat of last week's debacle!
I'm not worried though because she will forget one day, and I am remaining on high alert as you know.**

**Early this morning brought an old game into play as LD and I played "shall we poo or not" in the rain while Carrie pursued us with poo bags.
I often forget how much fun it is to see her in her pj's ducking under branches**

and being dripped on, while we pretend to find the perfect spot for our ablutions.
It can be quite a long game depending on how wet she is getting 

Enjoy the rain.

Lots of love,
Othello xxx

4th June 2020

Hello from Othello in rainy Wales!

We managed to get out for a walk before the rain set in.
We walked mostly on our leads this morning with a bit of drip feeding to distract us from a very speedy cyclist and some DMTing from a sheep with its lamb.

The trouble with going into the garden early in the morning, is that it leads to Carrie waving her arms around in the strangest way.
It took me a while to realise that she was trying to bat off the midges.

While she was behaving in what appeared to be a slightly possessed way, we got on with trying to locate the perfect toilet spot. I was first up with some very elegant foot work as I circled and sniffed and then relocated to repeat the process several times.
LD has a slightly more manic approach which involves lots of ducking around bushes and sniffing with a bit of leaf chasing, several trips back to the door to see if he can dash back in, and then a final decision over the ultimate location.

Have a lovely day.

Love from,
Othello xxx

Saw sheep.
Not bark.

Saw bike.
Not bark.

5th June 2020 Carrie into the online dog training group

Oberon is rocking being calm, in his pen with the gate open. The key to getting him there is to make everything around him super boring!
Seriously though, calm is a choice that would not be his first, but by focusing on calmness, he chooses it much more quickly these days. He's had no walk today yet, no games and nothing exciting happen. As a consequence, he's settled down and is currently snoring!
Ditto Othello.
Long may it last!

Lots of love,
Carrie xxx

The Oberon Stretch Gauge

Week 3

Running away feelings: Did not feel like running away even once.
Reduced to tears: Zero.
Laughs: Countless.
Recall: 90% He's starting to sometimes check out the environment before he rushes back, so I've upped the treat value and made myself look even more idiotic/exciting. 😁
Kibble: Ongoing battle. He doesn't like his own, but will eat Othello's if it's coated in cream cheese and wet dog food … sigh.

I feel he will need it coated in caviar and truffle oil soon. 😁
Mud incidents: Zero. There is little mud around, and the really muddy pond has only been passed while he's been on his lead. 👍
Resource guarding: Zero. Possibly due to management.
How many more puppies will I get? I have been very taken with the thought of a whippet one day. I took myself to one side and hit myself around the head with a newspaper until the thought dropped back out. 😁
Howling: Twice, when I had the bare-faced cheek to pretend I had the option to leave him alone and go outside with Othello. I did achieve it once by using smoke and mirrors, camouflage and full military operation guidelines 😁😁
It was only 10 minutes but it was bliss.
How much will I drink this weekend? My alter ego says to stop kidding myself and it's always going to be a bottle and a half. 😁😁
Still very little progress with being able to get time alone with Othello but it remains my dream. 💗

Lots of love,
Carrie xxx

6th June 2020

Carrie and I snuck out for a walk yesterday afternoon by leaving LD in the boot of the car in the shade. Jo was observing him at a distance, and he was as quiet as a sleeping mouse.
It was only about 20 minutes, but we had a blast!
We played ball for the first time in ages and it was the best fun ever.
I got so many hugs that I was embarrassed by it 😂😂

I don't like new things in old places but I didn't bark at the temporary sign in the road, because Carrie DMT'd it.

We're currently waiting for the rain to stop before we have another walk.
Happy weekend everyone.

Doggy Snuffles,
Othello xxx

Yesterday afternoon I did bark at a person on de track and run towards dem, but I did come back for treats.
I den walked with mys ead collar on for a while to calm down.
After dat we played running and jumping on logs and I ignored de person.

Wuv U

8th June 2020

We had a nice rummaging-around walk this morning.
I got to sniff at rabbit holes and dive into bushes, just for the fun of it.
I even managed to do a bit of tracking … not certain what I was tracking but it smelled good 😊

LD refused his breakfast, but BOY can he shift his butt when there are fish treats around.

Your friend,
Othello xxx

8th June 2020 Carrie into the online dog training group

So, for Oberon's next trick …
He refuses to eat his kibble, so I moved him to Othello's kibble which worked

for a little while but now he won't eat that. I've tried coating it with cream cheese, peanut butter, wet dog food and putting it in a licking bowl. That worked for a little while. But now he won't eat that either. Animating the food doesn't work. Putting it in toys doesn't work. Hand feeding doesn't work. Smacking my head against the wall doesn't work.
I've tried numerous types of kibble and he might take to a new one for a few days then he doesn't want that either. Needless to say, he will happily eat high value treats and enjoys licking a filled KONG for a short time.
I may just gather up all the sheep and horse poo and put that in his bowl because he loves that. 😂😂😂

Yours, frustratedly,
Carrie xxx

9th June 2020

I ave been to de groomer today.
I did bark.

Edit: The groomer said he howled, but he isn't admitting to that …
Carrie xxx

10th June 2020

Good morning!

Carrie and I have been up doing our morning workout.

I put a lot of energy into the experience.
However, I was soon regretting the outburst after realising that breakfast wasn't going to be happening any time soon 😟
I feel weak with hunger and I only hope I can summon up enough energy to get up when I hear the food bin open … sigh.

LD came back from the groomer yesterday smelling and looking like something most unpleasant.
Ridiculously, Carrie and Jo were cooing over him for ages saying how fluffy he was and how lovely he was smelling.
I can't understand the fuss, we all know proper dogs have short hair.
And that puppy has no self-respect – he kept rolling on his back and squirming and showing off his crown jewels.
This morning's target is to get him into as much mud as possible and wipe that smug look off his face 😂

Lots of love,
Othello xxx

Thello made I get in de river cos he said I waz stinky.
He sez I smellz better now.
I finks e is just mean though.

Wuv U

<u>11th June 2020</u>

Had a great start to the day with a few games, a Ruffle Snuffle mat and a licking mat.

All before LD got up.
Living the dream, that's me 😀

Then there was a tiny bit of confusion, mainly fuelled by Carrie not being clear that I wasn't supposed to be having a second breakfast.
Quite reasonably on my part I assumed the licking bowl on the floor contained a few extra morsels for me 😏
Carrie muttered something about it being in LD's pen so it was clearly for him and not me!
Anyway, she was the one that looked foolish because she prepared him another one for when he woke up and he didn't touch it!
Should have let me finish that one too 😂😂😂
I think he holds out so he can fill himself up on sheep poo.
I can always find a bit of room for that delicacy, but he's a picky eater 😏

We had to walk on our leads walks this morning, so sadly there was little adventure to be had, we behaved very well.
Apparently, I have to play some impulse-control games later, which I'm very good at but we all know in reality will make no difference if a licking bowl gets left around 😏😏
Have a great rest of your day.

Lots of love,
Othello xxx

I ave cided that I can only eat fish.
Nuffin else, just fish.
I iz wewy cute, so I fink I will win dis battle 😉

Wuv U

12th June 2020

The Oberon Stretch Gauge

Week 4

Running away feelings: Zero.
Reduced to tears: Zero.
Laughs: Countless.
Recall: 100% on the outward trip, 90% coming home as he is predicting the lead going back on! Stakes have been upped, higher value treats are being carried and lots of clipping the lead on and off. Most productive way of catching him is to sit in the middle of the track with my back to him. Hoping no neighbours come along and call the men with the straight jacket when they finally think I've lost the plot.
Kibble: As long as it has sardines mashed into it and it's rolled on the thighs of a virgin riding a Unicorn, he may give it a sniff or even eat a bit.
Mud incidents: A few more this week, but he had been to the groomer so he needed to "refresh" his smell.
Resource guarding: Once, when Othello decided to finish up his rejected kibble.
How many more puppies will I get! Depends how many the asylum will let me have.
Howling incidents: A couple, at the groomer's. I haven't been brave enough to offend him in any way that might provoke one this week.
How much will I drink this weekend? My alter ego refuses to narrow it down to the number of bottles as accidents happen.
Still working towards time alone with Othello.

Lots of love,
Carrie xxx

13th June 2020

Great start to the day, with Carrie doing "The dance of the entrails" first thing when she stepped in the gift the cats left her.

I made a move to get a second helping of the supplement powder when I saw LD's breakfast made up on the counter, but Carrie swooped in and stopped me. I'm guessing it's because if I got any more supple I'd tie myself in knots 😂😂

When we were out walking yesterday afternoon, I sat with my ball while Carrie was gawping at a load of army squaddies running by.
My gut feeling was that chasing them would help them to increase their fitness levels, but I controlled myself and waited patiently for Carrie's focus to return to me 😂😂
I'm still working on her focus as she is easily distracted 😉😉
Have a lovely weekend.

Slobbery kisses,
Othello xxx

<u>14th June 2020</u>

Othello here, in a very humid Wales.

LD and I had to DMT from a very sassy ram that came out from the grass verge earlier!
He was huge and fronted up to us, but even when he ran off, we just kept our focus on Carrie.
She stayed calm and remembered to give me my ball and treats to LD 😂
She also stayed focused enough to play a quick actual game of ball with me 😀😀
On another subject. I was super pleased that she'd put manure on the roses yesterday afternoon, as I got an unexpected evening snack 😉

Lots of love,
Othello xxx

Der was a big ram wiv big horns.

I did not bark.
I got treats.
I played in puddles.

Wuv U 

15th June 2020

Othello here in sunny Wales

We just had nice walk rummaging around and sniffing, with some Knicker Elastic game thrown in.

This morning was an on our leads walk with the rest of the gang.
It became a licking fest as the Youngest Boy was being silly and fell over so all five of us set about cleaning him up 😂
The more we licked the more he squirmed 😀😀

I have managed several times already today to tidy up the manure Carrie put on the roses (she is so forgetful that it's like taking candy from a baby 😂)

Sadly for The Youngest Boy, I did that after I licked him 😏

LD had a walk by himself earlier, so maybe I will get one later if it's not too sunny and he can be left in the car.

Slobbery kisses,
Othello xxx

Oberon here.
Some dogs did bark at I.
I did not bark.
I did come back wen Cawwie called I.
I iz a good boy, coz Cawwie sed.
I did play in mud.
😂
Wuv U 🐾🐾

16th June 2020 Carrie into the online dog training group

It's easy when you're living in the moment to forget how far you've come.

Othello and Oberon can, without a doubt, be a bit challenging sometimes, but they have both come a very long way.

Yesterday evening I left the house with them for an evening stroll. I hardly had hold of Othello's lead and immediately we were faced with a loose flock of sheep. Othello looked at them, and then straight back at me. I just said "niiice" and we continued walking as they ran off up the road in their sassy, come hither, way. Of course he got a treat, but he didn't really need it because he was cool with the situation. Oberon, being led by Jo, was certainly more interested in them but no pulling or barking, just watching.

A year ago, I would have left the house, feeling anxious, and clinging onto Othello's lead with a thumping heart, just praying that we came across no dogs, sheep, people, anything really. Not because he was aggressive but because he is very strong and if startled could bark and pull. The experience did not bring me joy. 😟
I got Oberon almost six months ago and he was scared of everything, a true pessimist who would whine incessantly on walks and bark at literally everything. Again, no joy in walking him. 😟

Skip forward to now and I am so proud of my boys. They aren't perfect but I

feel that we can handle most situations, because I've worked hard to get them more comfortable with what life throws at us. I'm also happy to say that we have a wonderful bond. 💗💗💗

Lots of love,
Carrie xxx

I am pretending to be asleep as I have been rather impulsive today 😉

Firstly, I ate LD's leftover breakfast when Carrie left the room.
I gobbled it so quickly that I was almost sick 😕
Carrie was cross with herself for forgetting to pick his food up, but she still gave me a really hard bear-stare and a telling of my fortune in a stern voice 🙊 I closed my ears when she said something about less dinner 😶

I do know she will forget about that, so I'm not actually worried 😁😁

Secondly, there was a bit of a muddy water hole incident and I was wearing my coat 😉
Apparently, the first time I went in was a lapse of good judgement but the second and third times were me just being a bit challenging 😂

I am going to lie here quietly until the dust settles 😂😂😂
If I'm lucky LD will do something to take the heat off me or I may be able to set him up 👍

Lots of love,
Othello xxx

I had a walk and den I got left in de pen wiv The Oldest Boy in de room looking after I.

Cawwie went outside wiv Thello.
I was sad, so I owled for a bit and did not eat de pigs ear she gave I.

Wuv U

<u>17th June 2020</u>

I have shown great impulse-control today!!
I did not eat Oberon's leftovers even though I feel that I'm doing him a great service if I do 😂😂
Let's face it, he does not want them!

I had a walk with Carrie, Jo and Truffles which was fabulous.
We left LD at home with one of the boys.
We played ball and I made sure that I shared it a little bit because I know it's good manners 😌
Not too much though because it is my ball.
I didn't bark at a wobbly lady, which I would have done last year, even though she was very interesting and very grumpy.

I was somewhat disappointed that Carrie avoided stepping in the mouse entrails this morning 😂
She's becoming a bit too nimble on her feet for my liking 😉
Have a lovely day everyone.

Yours, lovingly,
Othello xxx

I did not bark at dog.
It barked at I.
I saw de dog again and still did not bark.
It barked at I again.
I did not owl wen Cawwie went out wiv Thello.
I did splash in a puddle.
I did eat some breakfast.

Wuv U

18th June 2020

It's been raining and storming like crazy here.

I think because LD was already soaking wet, he thought that swimming in the muddy water hole was fine 😂

He found a dead Jay and was very scared of it so I showed him it was OK and then Carrie called us away.
I think LD might have run off with it if we'd stayed any longer 😟
I'm up for eating some treasures and even the odd shoulder-dip into unidentified poo but dead beasties are to be avoided 😟
They have a sad smell about them 😪

The good news is that LD does not appear to be scared of thunder. Carrie says it's because we live quite near the army firing range and he's used to big bangs.
I reckon he's just waiting to catch her off guard and then he'll go into full blown howling 😂😂

I did a little reconnaissance of LD's rejected breakfast, but sadly Carrie spotted me and gave me the hard bear-stare again 😒

Hoping to get some games in later.

Lots of love,
Othello xxx

I found what I fink waz a dead Ostrich, it was huge.
I waz not scared (don't listen to Thello).
I did not bark

Wuv U

<u>19th June 2020</u>

<u>The Oberon Stretch Gauge</u>

<u>Week 5</u>

Running away feelings: Zero. 👍
Reduced to tears: Zero.
Laughs: Countless.
Recall: 100%
Kibble: Sigh … sadly, the Unicorn artist left after complaining that she didn't feel valued enough, and as yet there has been no response to the advert I placed in a national newspaper for a replacement. I can see her point as she spent a lot of time rolling fish for the recipient to just walk away in disgust. Sardines have crept down the list of things Oberon will eat.
Mud incidents: What can I say? The boy's just gotta have fun.
Resource guarding: Zero.
How many more puppies will I get? I stand by last week's statement. 😉
Howling incidents: One, when he knew I was outside with Othello (I didn't

repeat that mistake). I did manage to take Othello for a walk without him but we both had to slowly crawl to the door, holding our breath and commando roll out the front door.
How much will I drink this weekend? Not much as I'm currently saving to pay the footman who will no doubt shortly be required to serve Oberon's food on a silver salver.
Have achieved some 1-2-1 with Othello. 🎉🎉
Happy weekend everyone.

Lots of love,
Carrie xxx

20th June 2020

Fanfare time 🎉

I got "Terry Time" yesterday!!
I know, I know, you can feel the excitement already!!
As soon as I saw his car I very nearly combusted with anticipation! 😀😀😀
Carrie opened the crate and I shot out of the boot and nearly knocked her over.
I haven't seen my hero for weeks and weeks!!!
All the time we walked I was just trotting along and bouncing about, waiting for a moment's attention from him.
I was so excited that I have no idea if Carrie and LD were even there!
He threw sticks into ponds for me and his three dogs which was amazing (as I'm not allowed sticks).
He also threw stones into the river (I'm not allowed those either).
I'm breathless with joy just remembering it … sigh 😀😀
Carrie almost had to shoehorn me back into the car 😂😂

Yours, happily,
Othello xxx

I saw dat Terry guy and his dogs.
Dont know what Thello sees in im.
I wike his dogs though cos dey do run and jump wiv I.
I did bark.
And I did bark some more.
Terrys dogs barked too.
I wuv Cawwie better dan Thello does 💗💗💗

Wuv U

21st June 2020 Carrie into the online dog training group

I had a very proud moment yesterday afternoon! Othello and Truffles saw two loose sheep before I did. They looked straight back at me and then ran to me before I said a word. They did that all in a split second. That dreadful split second where everything can go wrong. Truffle's instinct is always to be on the alert for sheep. She's from working stock and it took me years to train her not to follow her instinct, but her collie eye remains ready, just in case. It's fair to say that Truffles followed Othello's example. More and more, I'm seeing that he is making the right decision before I've reacted in any way. Oberon didn't see the sheep as he was on his lead after starting a barking fest with Truffles. 😕

Lots of love,
Carrie xxx

22nd June 2020

After lots of Ninja activity, Carrie and I got out for a walk without LD.

She put him in the crate in the car and we tiptoed out of the garden holding our breath.
We only managed to get about a mile in total though because Carrie got stopped five times by people wanting to chat to her! Yawn!
By the end I was doing my most pitiful whines, because I wanted to get moving.
I did get lots of treats drip fed to me though, so I don't feel too hard done by 😀

Loads of novelty stuff out there today which helps to keep Carrie on her toes.

A woman with a pushchair and a child on a bike (obviously the pushchair and the child were not both on the bike, although that would have been very novel 😂).

A Photographer with a huge camera. He jawed for ages about Pine martens, whatever they might be.
I'm confident that I can't eat one though, so I wasn't that interested.

A man up a ladder using a big noisy machine. I have no idea what he was doing but he felt the need to stop and interrupt my walk.
I thought about cocking my leg on his ladder but sensed that Carrie would give me a look, so I reconsidered 😉

Two different men stopped in their vans to chat about nothing interesting.
I poked my head through their windows and checked to see if they had any food to snaffle, but they didn't have a scrap.
One of them tried to butter me up with talk of how handsome I am, but they had no snacks to back it up, so I cold-shouldered them.

It was nice to be out with Carrie though.

Lots of love,
Othello xxx

22nd June 2020

Today I waz supposed to sit on a bench.
I did not do it.
I just jumped on and jumped off.
Den I ran round and round it.
I ate some grass.
I ad to do some Figure of Eight walking.

Cawwie sez I iz crazy today.

Wuv U

23rd June 2020

It's very hot here today, so I'm making the most of the cool sofa.

Carrie is puzzling over me today because I have been ignoring loose sheep again, and although I'm very happy to take the treats when she's saying Niiiice, if I'm honest, I don't need them.
She hadn't realised yet that it's because she's so much more relaxed 😂
Obviously if they stared at me it would be a bit different because I hate sheep or dogs staring at me! Then she'd have do some serious DMTing or offer me something really tasty 😂😂

The man was up the ladder again and called out to us, so I considered barking at him but frankly it was too hot to bother.
He wanted to talk to her about something, so she left me, LD and Truffles with Jo on the other side of the road.
LD didn't whine or make a fuss, but I did big whines 'cos I didn't like her talking to a strange man 😞

I was very helpful earlier and did a bit of tidying up of cat food but I don't think Carrie noticed 😏
Have a lovely day.

Lots of love,
Othello xxx

I ave not eaten mys breakfast.
I do not wike sardines anymore.
I was spposed to put two paws on a tree.
I played in mud instead 😄

24th June 2020

I'm sitting in the dark trying to get cool.

We went for a walk and there were lots of rams in the field giving me the evils. As you know, I do not like sheep staring at me and I have barked at them before, but I decided to do a different behaviour and I ate their poo instead 😂😂😂
I'm not entirely sure that it was the alternative behaviour that Carrie was looking for but she should learn to be a bit more grateful.
She was a bit rude and said something about me not needing much food later!

That's not going to happen though as I have a few, yet undiscovered, tricks up my leg 😏

I had to do those silly leg weaves that make Carrie look like she's got uncomfortable undercrackers on 😂😂

Stay cool,

Love,
Othello xxx

Itz wewy hot.
Leg weaves made I even hotter.
I saw some dogs.
I did not bark.
Saw sheep.
Did not bark.
Saw horses.
Did not bark.
Cawwie left I and went outside wiv Thello.
I did bark.

Wuv U

25th June 2020 Carrie into online dog training group

Here's to the people I call "My Tribe"
With "challenging" dogs that reach far and wide
The people who catch me when I take a fall
The people who cheer me to walk ten feet tall
The people who praise us when we get it right
The people who make it feel less of a fight
The people who hear me when I have a struggle
The people who send me a huge virtual cuddle
Here's to the dogs who brought us all here
Their barking, their howling, their "irrational" fears
Their crazy behaviour that keeps us all busy
Their whirling and jumping that sends us all dizzy
Here's to the numerous "Powerful Whys"
That brought us all here to open our eyes
Here's to the chieftains, Lauren and Tom
For creating a tribe that brought us all home. 💕

Lots of love
Carrie xxx

We had great fun in the river last night.
LD ran off with the Jo's sock when she took it off to paddle, and then Jo and The Youngest Boy had a pretend fight and both fell in 😂

I haven't had a walk today because it's too hot, but I've had a play in the paddling pool and I spent some time checking out the agility tunnel for snacks. I was disappointed to find it empty 😔
Carrie said it only has treats when the sun isn't shining so I should be OK for about 360 days of the year 😂😂

Stay cool everyone.

Love from,
Othello xxx

Did you know that u don't ave to go indoorz wen u iz asked?
I do now!

Wuv U 

26th June 2020

The Oberon Stretch Gauge

Week 6

Running away feelings: Monday and Tuesday I could have cheerfully skipped off into the sunset with Othello.
Reduced to tears: Once, though frustration … more details to follow
Laughs: Countless, particularly with his new-found pleasure which is to go to the top of a leafy, twiggy, bank and roll down it … repeatedly , thus ensuring that every single piece of debris is tightly embedded in his curls.
Recall: This week this a concept that LD imagines is meant for other dogs only.
Kibble: Here lie the tears of frustration.
Sardines are "so last week", kibble has literally become luck of the draw. Huge dog biscuits are the best thing in the world, but only if I present one wearing a Tiara and gown, with a flip flop on one foot, a wellie on the other and sing Hound Dog while gyrating my hips and curling my lip.
No need to continue the search for a Unicorn rider as I am rocking the artistic stuff myself.
Mud incidents: Numerous, but his joy is such a pleasure to behold.
Resource guarding: Zero.
How many more puppies will I have? Perhaps he needs one to keep him

company. 😁😁😁😁😁😁😁
Howling incidents: There have been a fair few 😥 I have managed a couple of short walks with Othello, while Oberon stayed in the car, so no commando rolling has been required this week – although Othello did recommend I try going commando after feeling that my terrible leg weave moves were associated with tangled undergarments. 🙊
How much wine will I drink this weekend: Still saving for Henry the Footman but I think there's a dusty bottle of sweet sherry somewhere. 😱
Happy weekend everyone!!

Lots of love,
Carrie xxx

28th June 2020

Morning from Othello and Oberon!

We will be working on calmness today as Carrie got a bit over-excited in bed this morning 😏😏😏
Turns out that she thought the roof was leaking when she felt something wet drop onto her wrist, but it wasn't water it was a slug 😂😂😂😂
That's what happens if you sleep with your window open 😂😂😂😂
She said that is just goes to show how quickly your emotions can switch from fear to disgust and still no one knows why you're making a fuss 😂😂😂
A bit like us dogs with our "crazy" behaviour 😏😏

Love from,
Your friend,
Othello xxx

29th June 2020

This morning is a nightmare!!!

All the training that I've put in with Carrie has just gone out the window!!

She's been dancing up and down the kitchen making squeaking noises, and when she's not doing that she giggling at her tablet.
I've tried calmness games but unfortunately LD is buying into the stupidity too and he's dancing around like a fool.
I can not get her to disengage from the screen whatever I try 😟
There will definitely be no walking today until she calms down.
This inappropriate behaviour seems to be associated with something about studying to be a Pro Dog Trainer (PDT) and then some Geeky learning course 😂😂😂

Yours, despairingly,
Othello xxx

30th June 2020

I did not bark at barky dog.
I did not bark at horses.
I played fun stuff wiv Cawwie.
I did owl in de car.

Good morning from Othello in drizzly Wales.

I took Carrie for a walk this morning as she was over-excited in the house.
I know that I should have let her calm down a bit more, but frankly I needed a break from her over-excitement.
She was away with the fairies, and almost jumped out of her skin when a dog barked at us through a fence.
Needless to say, I did not react, and luckily, she remembered her training and gave me treats.

We played ball for a while, and some other games, as I didn't want her running off anywhere.

On the way back she stood jawing to someone for ages.
In the end I just lay down having resigned myself to a very long wait.
It wasn't a complete waste of time though, as she kept dropping treats to me 😀

I did get bored after a while though, so I barked at a cat that crossed the road 😂😂😂
That seemed to spur her into action, and we came home.

Apparently, LD had been howling while we were out and now he's over-excited too ... sigh!

Lots of love,
Othello xxx

Chapter Ten
'Sardines, sheep and fishy treats'

1st July 2020

Frankly, I think LD was dropped on his head as a tiny puppy.

Here are just two reasons why I think this:

1: His strange obsession with Carrie.
We all know that she's one banana short of a bunch, but he seems to think that she's some sort of icon.
Now if she was bacon, I would understand 😂😂

2: The way he picks at his food! Now I am an enthusiastic eater (something that Carrie and I have in common 😌) but he turns his nose up at just about everything.
This morning he had fish mashed into his kibble (to make it all softy wofty for the little baby 😈) and he wouldn't eat it!!

To rub salt into the wound I'm on a diet and not allowed to touch it … grrrr!
Be honest, do think you my bum is big?
My tummy is rumbling and if I try to pick up a few tiny morsels when we're out then I get the bear-stare.

Yesterday I was trying to eat grass, which has no calories, but I was in trouble

for that too! Something about vomiting it back up in the night!! As if!!
To be honest, that is a fun game and sometimes if I can't sleep I play that.
It's my version of Carrie's Knicker Elastic game, I count how long it takes for her to wake up and leap out of bed 😂😂😂😂

I have not given up on snaffling LD's leftovers though, as they are still within my reach if I stand on tippy toes and stretch hard.

If all else fails then I will check underneath the sofa, as there are always a few lonely biscuits amongst the dust bunnies.

Talking of which, I haven't checked in front of the rabbit cage yet today!!
Off to do that now!

Your friend with the rumbly tummy,
Othello xxx

I did not wike mys breakfast so I did not eat it.
Thello iz welcome to it!

Wuv U

2nd July 2020

So much for the thought that calmness breeds calmness!!

I have been virtually comatose since Carrie started studying to become a dog trainer, lying on my bed and setting a great example.
I'm trying to bring her excitement levels down, but every time I think I'm making progress she starts behaving badly again.

If I'd known that studying would make her so out of control, I would have stopped her joining the courses!

First thing this morning we did a very relaxing workout together.
I interrupted her whenever I saw that she was tipping towards any silly behaviour, by lying next to her and breathing deeply.
I could tell that I was making some progress and was hoping we had finally turned a corner, then she looked at her tablet and that was it – crazy excitement again.
Something to do with a box of goodies coming in the post to help with the training courses.

I'm seriously thinking of booking a consult with Dr. Tom Mitchell 😂😂

Incidentally, I managed a successful rummage behind the dog food bins yesterday and was able to stave off the hunger pangs.

Lots of love,
Othello xxx

3rd July 2020 Carrie into online dog training group

The Oberon Stretch Gauge

Week 7

Running away feelings: "Brisk walking away" feelings once or twice. 😉
Reduced to tears: Zero.
Laughs: Countless. Seeing him chasing a leaf around the garden is guaranteed to make me laugh 😀, along with his cute little smile and cartoon dog running.
Recall: He seems to have remembered that it's him I'm calling rather than some random dog with the same name. 😂
Kibble:

Monday: It was OK if mashed into fishy dog food with a silver fork.
Tuesday: Hated fishy dog food but quite liked sardines as long as they were in virgin olive oil (it felt like there might be a virgin theme going so I rolled with it, slightly regretting the loss of our friend from Unicorn Land. I penned a letter to her pleading for a relative to be dispatched promptly).
Wednesday: Took long stick and hooked letter back out of post box as sardines are off the menu again.
Thursday: Little fish-shaped dog treats were particularly nice but only if fed individually while I wore white gloves and sang "When the boat comes in".
Friday: Currently sticking the torn-up letter back together. 😉😉😉

Mud incidents: On the bright side, light coloured carpets go darker really quickly and you soon forget their original colour. 😁
Resource guarding: Zero.
How many more puppies will I have: Obviously none as I will be too busy studying. Having a new puppy to work with would be just too much. 😂😂😂😂
Howling incidents: What had previously been a "no howling zone", the crate in the car, has now become a favourite howling place. Presumably because of the acoustics. 🙄
How much wine will I drink this weekend: Honestly? Still saving for the footman, but I think I might indulge in a glass or two. 😂😂

So poor Othello has had limited 1-2-1 time 😒

Meanwhile, even though hubby has been able to hear the little darling howling from his office, tensions are clearly not as high as I believed. He asked some really nice men to pop around with a gift for me. They were keen for me to try it on while they were here and it was a lovely white linen jacket with wrap-around arms. I don't know what hubby was thinking of, buying it in white, I didn't even get married in white because I didn't want to blend in with all the other kitchen appliances. Anyway, I thanked them politely and suggested they take it away and rethink the colour.
If they bring it back in purple we can talk again.
Have a lovely weekend. 😘😘

Lots of Love,
Carrie xxx

4th July 2020

**Even though it's drizzling I've already had an amazing start to the day.
Carrie and I woke up at what we call "sparrow fart" and used our very quiet commando moves to escape the bedroom without LD noticing (he was still snoring in his crate).**

**Let the fun begin!
We left the house with a skip in our step and made our way briskly to the forest.
The ball came out and I went into seventh heaven!
We played loads of fetching the ball back to 'almost' Middle (I like to drop it before I go into Middle 😂), Knicker Elastic and diving into water pools (me not Carrie).**

We were both surprised when a man and his collie appeared from around a corner, but we recovered quickly and went straight back to ball playing.

**LD is still asleep and I'm off for a snooze too.
Happy Saturday.**

**Lots of love,
Othello xxx**

5th July 2020

Sum xciting fings appened today.

I went in de car to a big pet shop.
Iz de first time in 3 months coz of some virus fing.

I Sniffed at de nice smellz.
I vomited on de floor.
Came home.

Wuv U

6th July 2020

Well, it's raining again which meant LD wore his silly coat when we went walking.
Can't see the point really because he still dives into the water holes and mud wearing it 😂

We went on a road trip yesterday, and I'm pleased to say that I now have a hammock to sit in on the back seat of the car.
No more sharing the crate in the boot with Moany-pants.
I don't think he'll be happy when he works out where I am sitting, so don't tell him 😉

On a sombre note, we had a family bereavement yesterday, The Youngest Boy's mouse died.
There was a lot of effort put into making a tiny boat, so it could have a viking burial on the river.
Once it had set sail, I wasn't allowed to go and retrieve the boat which seemed a bit unfair.
However the river was very rough and, suffice to say, after much shenanigans and worry that the boat might sink, the mouse had a garden burial in the end 😂
The spot has been marked, presumably to make it easier for the cats to dig it back up 😂

Yours, sadly,
Othello xxx

7th July 2020

My day started with a bit of attempted nursing.
I tried very hard to lick a little mole back to life, but sadly my efforts were wasted.
I love most little animals and I was a bit gloomy about its demise.

The cats had clearly been on a hunt during the night.
Another sacrifice on the funeral pyre 😞

Yesterday evening we went to the river and played swimming games and hide and seek.
Truffles and I had to find Carrie and LD.
They went off, leaving us with The Youngest Boy and Jo. It was a bit head-spinning because Truffles, being a collie, likes to round the family back up so we were dashing between Carrie and LD and The Youngest Boy and Jo.
The river was great fun and I would have happily stayed in it, but Truffles enthusiasm does rub off so I helped her chase after Carrie and LD 😂
It was worth it for the fish treats though 😀
LD, being a mummy's boy, just wanted to stay with Carrie, so he didn't join in the dashing game.
We all had another swim in the river on the way home, and LD did his rolling down the bank collecting up twigs and moss in his fur.

It's not raining today so I predict more outside fun 😊

Your friend,
Othello xxx

8th July 2020

I waz spposed to be sitting on a log.
Didnt though.
Cawwie got us lost in de woods.
We had to fend for ourselves for agez.

Good job der waz no bears.
I waz wewy brave 😀
We played and I got sprats.

Wuv U

9th July 2020

I had a few minutes 1-2-1 with Carrie this morning which I thought was lovely.

Sadly, LD did not think it was lovely even though he was left with a treat that I would have loved.
He quickly went into howl mode 😞
I noticed that he hadn't eaten his chew when we came in so I'm hoping to snaffle it later.

We played a few games while we were outside including one of my favourites.
It's hide and and seek with treats.
We wait for Carrie to hide them and then use our snozzles to sniff them out.

I have more impulse-control with that than I do with cat food 😂😂
Although, to be fair, my impulse-control mostly depends on whether Carrie is watching or not 😇
It's hardly surprising that I do the odd bit of clearing up, as Carrie still has me on starvation rations.
Apparently, I'm still a bit thick around the waist.
Methinks she is projecting and in no place to comment!
Have a great day

Love from,
Othello xxx

10th July 2020 Carrie into online dog training group

The Oberon stretch gauge

Week 8

Running away feelings: Not precisely, but some going to the very end of the garden and practising my "Square Words" as my daughter used to call them. 😂
Reduced to tears: Very nearly, but I reminded myself that it wasn't stress, just a means of testing my strength of character. 😉
Laughs: Countless, the boy is part howler monkey and part comedian.
Recall: 99% There was one tricky moment in the garden where I felt like Kevin Costner's stand in for Dances with Wolves. He went one way, I went the other. I called sweet endearing words in a cheerful tone and he leapt about with the stuffing from a dismembered toy. Hysterical laughter on my part is no longer novel, but the sight of me curled up in a ball, groaning, finally lit his curiosity and all was well.
Kibble: Thinking that we may need to create another exit from the house as the bags of "liked yesterday" kibble is becoming too tall to climb over. Sadly, no reply from relative of the Unicorn artist.
Mud incidents: Successful DMTing from puddles of less than 1" depth. Anything deeper leads to intermittent deafness. Note to myself to research the science behind deafness and mud.
Resource guarding: Zero.
How many more puppies will I have: Just popping to the end of the garden for a while.
Howling incidents: Any attempts to outwit LD in order to spend time with Othello have failed. Previously-used tactic of daughter "vanishing" Othello to the garden while I sing a lullaby, prior to sauntering from room, has been sussed. Ear defenders purchased for entire household in case the desire to study entices me to bend against LD's will.
How much wine will I drink this weekend: Tbh, feeling a little jaded this morning as I mistakenly thought yesterday was Friday. 😉😂
Happy weekend everyone. 😘😘

Lots of love,
Carrie xxx

11th July 2020

Oberon here.
I wike sniffing.
I wike eating grass,
I wike Cawwie and her treats.

Wuv U

12th July 2020

Carrie has a bee in her bonnet today about us needing extra training, so we've been working hard for our food.

We are going to the river in a minute but I suspect falling in might dampen her ardour 😂😂😂

Not that I would instigate such a thing, but I have found that unpredicted "Middle" can throw her off balance 😂
I will keep you updated.

Doggy kisses,
Othello xxx

13th July 2020

Morning from Othello!

Sadly, Carrie did not fall in yesterday, despite my very best efforts!
Truffles collected stones from the river and put them on the bank while LD pretended to be a Kangaroo and bounced around in the water.

Today we have been practising reacting to everything.
Carrie did not realise that when she chose the caravan as her office, that it would introduce us to a whole new level of interesting noises … the bin men coming, the farmer's noisy machines driving by, branches knocking against its side.
It's so much closer to the road, so even people walking by can be very interesting.
Loads of opportunity for practising DMT and more treats for us.
It all helps with her training so I think she must be very pleased with us 😊

Life is good,
Othello xxx

14th July 2020

This morning's walk was very exciting.

We both ignored two loose sheep, which was worth some very yummy treats.

I must admit that I had some difficulty leaving the tantalising smell on a deer trail.
However, I did my duty, in order to assist with Carrie's training, and came back when I was called and was rewarded with some dried sprats 😀

We did loads of chasing after Carrie when she randomly ran off.
I've decided that perhaps Carrie is right, I do need to shed an ounce or two as LD keeps beating me back to Carrie 😂😂

We came across a new dog on the track and I'm sorry to say that Carrie was in a

daze (dreaming of something frivolous no doubt) so we got to say hello before she noticed (her bad!).
I recalled but LD was doing his silly puppy wriggling around it so Carrie had to apologise and put him on his lead.
I think she has learned a valuable lesson about day dreaming 😂

Your friend,
Othello xxx

We saw sheep.
Not xciting, I ave seen sheep before.
I went in puddles.
Saw a new dog.
I waz wewy interested in it.
I had to go on mys lead😞

Wuv U

15th July 2020

We had a walk without LD this morning!!!

He was being held hostage at home by Jo.

We skipped off into the drizzly forests for some fun time.
Ball, Mouse, Two Paws On, Middle and Toy Switch.

I had a nice swim in a muddy water hole which apparently wasn't part of the plan, but I was keeping life interesting 😂😂

I would have preferred the river, but I knew that there was no way I would make it there without being recalled 😂😂

I have to work with what I've got!
Tweaking any plan to get the best from it is essential, so I'm sure Carrie must see the benefits.
My coat won't remain shiny if I don't have at least one mud bath each week.

Yours, contentedly,
Othello xxx

16th July 2020

I saw a big helicopter.
It flew over mys ead.
I did not bark.
I waz brave🖤

Wuv U

17th July 2020 Carrie into online dog training group

The Oberon Stretch Gauge

Week 9

Running away feelings: Zero … don't want to miss out on my studies and I haven't yet found a tree in the forest with a charging point for my tablet.
Reduced to tears: Zero. Whoop!
Laughs: Countless.
Recall: We had a tricky moment when he decided to go into full blown

wriggle mode with a smidgen of bouncy fun because he saw a potential new friend. My encouraging calls fell on deaf ears. Red-faced and apologetic I explained that "I was just looking after him for someone else" 😂😂 (A friend used to say she was the Nanny if her children misbehaved in public, so it tripped off my tongue😉) A few under-the-breath Square Words were emitted once I had danced around him and his new friend while trying to grab his collar. The other dog's owner gave me the pitying look that is exclusive to those with perfect dogs. 😂 I wished her only charitable thoughts as I attempted to encourage LD away with high value treats and loving tones (that he could undoubtedly see through). She continued to gaze at me with the knowledge that her Amethyst would never behave in such a disgraceful way. Actually, I lie; if my wishes came true then her perfect pup was rolling in fox poo shortly after our encounter and smearing it into her immaculate beige trousers. 😉 I am only human after all. 😉😉
Kibble: Not much to report here. No news from Unicorn Land, so I slog on with my fruitless attempts to make food more interesting. Suffice to say the Youngest Boy thought it was funny for Oberon to eat kibble from his ear once, but was not prepared to the commit to the cause full time. Perhaps me filming it to add to his 18th Birthday collection may have been the decider? I thought I was on to a winner when I mashed some dog food, from a well-known supermarket, into his kibble and he wolfed it down. However, he must have read the label because he refused it next time. 😕
Resource guarding: Zero.
Mud incidents: There have been a few, but I laugh them off and remind myself that "dogs must be allowed to be dogs". 😂😂 In all honesty his happiness is just infectious, each time he splashes he does it with the joy of a new discovery. 😊
How many more puppies will I get: A nice "easy to train" Afghan would clearly suit the environment I live in. 😂
Howling incidents: Sadly, he has howled a few times.
How much wine will I drink?: Off on holiday tomorrow so freaking loads. 😂

Can't wait to see what Oberon thinks of a week by the sea!

Happy Weekend. 😘😘😘

Lots of love,
Carrie xxx

19th July 2020

We are on holiday, whatever that is!

**I'm currently having an after-breakfast relax.
A scatter feed was the start of the day for me.
The garden here is full of great smells and a bird table for after-breakfast snacks 😂😂**

**I managed to help out because The Youngest Boy had left the bag of dog food close to the edge of the worktop.
I emptied it a bit to balance its centre of gravity.
Not sure that Carrie appreciated my effort though ... sigh.**

**Someone has put a lovely white drinking fountain for dogs in the bathroom.
It's just at my height which is fab.
It's right next to the toilet, so if the lid is down on that then I don't have to worry about being thirsty 😂😂😂
I've been trying to work out how to use it by myself and hope to master it soon.**

Hope to introduce LD to the sea today 😂😂

**Lot's of love from,
Othello xxx**

20th July 2020

We went to the beach this morning, really early.

**LD thinks the sea is just another puddle to splash around in.
He loved swimming and finding seaweed to stick his nose in 😀
I had a blast swimming after the frisbee and running up and down the beach.**

There was a man swimming in the sea with what looked like a big ball attached to him but apparently it wasn't for chasing.
Carrie said it was a float.
I could tell it was afloat because it wasn't sinking!!

There were some seagulls sat on a wall which I have to be honest and say we both barked at when they flapped their wings. I even did a bit of a pull

Yours, salty dog,
Othello xxx

Saw sea.
Swam in it.
Saw big birds.
I did bark at dem.
Dey barked back

Wuv U

21st July 2020

More fun at the beach
Frisbee galore … Swimming to make my heart burst
The sea is the best place in the world.
LD gets very excited, but Carrie says "If a boy can't bark at the beach then there are too many rules"
We're loving the relaxed attitude she has!

Yours, happily,
Othello xxx

Did run.
Did bark.
Did swim.
Did wike it.

Wuv U

22nd July 2020

Morning!
I had a nice swim in de sea.
I did not wike the sound of the sea banging against de rocks 😨
I did wike another dog and I did run after it, but I came back 😄

Wuv U

23rd July 2020

Luckily, Carrie did not put on a wetsuit again.
I was worried that a shark might come and eat her with all the thrashing around she was doing in the sea yesterday 😂😂

I am still not a fan of seagulls.

They are very big, noisy and flappy things, so I'm glad we don't have them at home.

Talking of birds, Carrie filled up the bird feeders today so I will be tidying up under them later 😂
There is also a big compost bin here which smells amazing.
Something goes in there at night and rummages around, so I've found a few tasty morsels around it too.

The beach in the morning is also a good place for the odd tasty snack. People don't clear up properly after their evening fun so there a leftovers around😁
I take my job as a tidying dog very seriously 😉
Of course, if I wasn't on starvation rations I wouldn't need to scavenge to keep the hunger pangs away 😁

It's started to rain hard so I'm not sure what fun we will find today.

There has been a pigeon marching about on the conservatory roof in the mornings. We've both enjoyed barking at him, but he is clearly afraid of rain and has stayed away today.
Either that or we've scared him off 😂
It's worth barking at it for the DMT treats though 😂

Have a good day

Love from,
Othello xxx

24th July 2020 Carrie into online dog training group

The Oberon Stretch Gauge

Week 10

"The Holiday"
Running away: Zero!! Holiday has been bliss.
Reduced to tears: Zero.
Laughs: Countless!! Every stone on the beach was "the one" that LD needed most. They needed to be sniffed, licked, and carried around. Seaweed is a delight that cannot be disengaged from but in the sweetest way. An ant's nest was mind-blowing for him as they were scurrying everywhere, and he had no idea which way to turn. Luckily, he didn't get bitten!
Recall: This proved to be tougher than I imagined as there was so much exciting stuff going on, so I've sometimes employed the longline to save him making the wrong choices. With fewer distractions his recall has been perfect.
Kibble: He has settled on tinned dog food and sardines for this week. Kibble is no longer acceptable in any form. On the plus side he is eating. No need for any Unicorn riders at the moment, but I won't call off the search just yet.
Mud: He laughs in the face of mud!! It's nothing compared with wet, sticky, oily, sand. It's a perfect accompaniment to seaweed, to massage deep into the skin with a few shoulder-dipping moves. The smell is a wonder to be enjoyed at your leisure. To finish the performance off to perfection the car crate bed needs to be employed to trap and absorb the smelly delight. It's guaranteed I will forget to wash it before the next outing so we get to enjoy the smell several times over
Resource guarding: Zero.
How many more puppies will I get: Holidays give us rose tinted glasses.
Wine: What can I say? I'm on holiday.

Othello has been a delight as always, and I am ever thankful that I have him in my life (Oberon most of the time too).
Oberon has proved himself to be a star this week in so many ways. He has not barked at any of the dogs who have barked at him. He has seen tractors, buggies, bikes, joggers, screaming children, the sea and many more things, repeatedly, and just taken them in his stride. He did bark at a seagull, probably because Othello did, but in general, no signs of overwhelm at all. He has looked at everything, sometimes taken time to focus back on me, but no other reaction. He slept in his crate beautifully at night and used his boundary perfectly.

My gorgeous Othello went home with Jo yesterday. That was a tough decision for me, as being without him is like missing a limb. It has given me the opportunity to observe Oberon's behaviour without him. I wondered how much of Oberon's confidence was coming from Othello's presence. It seems like very little though. I've walked Oberon mostly on his own this week, apart from beach trips, and I have been impressed, astonished and deeply proud of him. 🤩😍🖤🖤🖤🖤
Looking forward to seeing my wonderful Othello tomorrow morning. 

Lots of love,
Carrie xxx

25th July 2020

"The Holiday" was just wonderful.

The sea is one of my very favourite places and it was great to introduce LD to it. Luckily, my fur is very good for shaking out the sand 😁 unlike LD's which is basically a muck trap. He has been a right little stinker at times 😂🤢

I have to say that, although I loved being away on holiday there are bonuses to being home again:
1. I get to sit in one of my favourite places and stare out of the window into the field. Eventually a cat will appear and I do an under my breath moan, which means Carrie says "niiice" and gives me a treat.
Repeat, repeat, repeat 😉 What's not to love?
2. As we haven't seen one for a week, Carrie has forgotten about the little nuggets of joy that sheep leave behind, so I've had lots of ground snacks this afternoon 😁
3. Since we've been away some new ditches have been dug in the forest, so I've had the opportunity take in a full body spa 😉
I'm living the dream 😂😉

Lots of love,
Othello xxx

<u>26th July 2020</u>

Good Afternoon!

Carrie is in one of her moving furniture moods, so our raised beds ended up the wrong way up!!
We didn't care though because we are very good at improvising, so we just slept on them while they were upside down!

I've played a few games this morning for my tiny amount of food allowance, hence my need to lie down and rest.
I'm positively weak with hunger 😉

We're off for a gallop around the woods as soon as the rain stops. My plan is to dart off ahead and get treats for coming back 😁

Your friend,
Othello xxx

Mr Knotty has been in mys fur again.
Cawwie sez I ave half de beach stuck in it 😄😄😱
I ave been groomed and I fell asleep til it got too tuggy 😟😕

Wuv U

<u>27th July 2020</u>

Good Morning,

It's Monday again, and time for Carrie to get Carried Away (!) writing in her notebook because of this weird PDT thing.
I think it stands for Please Don't Talk, because every time we go to say something we get interrupted 😂😂😂

We were mostly lying on our beds which is fab because she keeps throwing treats to us for literally nothing.

We're finally off for a walk now!

Lots of love,
Othello xxx

28th July 2020

Good morning!

Carrie started her day off as usual with lots of rolling around on the floor waving her arms and legs in the air and a whole heap of grunting while she was lifting weights.
I tried sitting on her at one point, as I really thought she was in need of some calmness exercises.
I also tried to lick the sweat from her brow, but she wasn't keen! 😂😂
There is no helping some people!

She has got a bit rotund during the holiday, so you'll be please to know that she's on starvation rations too 😂😂
Of course it's really justified with her, unlike poor me. I'm just a few ounces over weight 😉
I swear I could hardly sleep last night for my tummy rumbling 😌

Carrie's head is still in the holiday zone and I managed the odd sheep nugget yesterday evening while she was daydreaming 😂😂. Without those I may well have collapsed from hunger.

When she pops outside in a minute, I will do a quick patrol of the cat's bowls and a mooch around the rabbit's house but don't say anything ... shhhh! 😉

Yours, hungrily,
Othello xxx

29th July 2020

Afternoon!

Well, that's me done for the day!
This learning that Carrie is doing seems to require a lot of input from me, which is interrupting my much-needed sleep when new games have to be tried out.

Apparently, I need to be more flexible in my thinking and things that would normally be part of my routine need to be changed.
To be honest, I'm wondering if that's just an excuse and this supposed lack of flexibility is another dig at my increased waist size and the fact that I can't reach my toes so easily 😁

I have decided to take a nap and ignore anything that happens unless there is food involved 😂😃

Lots of love,
Othello xxx

I found a stick.
I did chew de stick.

I saw dogs.
I did not bark.

Wuv U

29th July 2020 Carrie into the online dog training group

Very, very, long post alert!!
Time to share a fabulous win!!
As those of you who have been here for a while know, Othello is the keeper of my heart and to me the best dog in the world. 💕 Walking with him is one of my greatest pleasures in life and lifts my spirits and touches my soul.
Oberon (LD) came to me initially as an unexpected visitor, and then as a permanent resident, just before Christmas last year. He came with a boat-load of anxieties, stomach issues, resource guarding and a few other issues. To say he is a Velcro dog would be an understatement; he sticks to me every second that he can. He can sometimes cope for a small period with just Othello, depending on what I am doing, but both of us being gone would cause his world to collapse. 😱
All that said, he is so loving, bright and full-on-enthusiastic about life. I adore the little boy, although I've shed many a tear of frustration because of his "issues".
I had a consultation with Dr. Tom Mitchell, which gave me huge insight into what makes this boy tick, and we have made massive progress with 95% of the struggles. We are just working on that last 5% now.
Last week we were on holiday. Rather than the usual "throw Othello's bed and food in the car", taking Oberon was a logistical nightmare of; a variety of different foods (his taste changes from day to day); which crate to take (if I take his night crate and he gets upset will I corrupt its use at home?); ditto his crate bed and raised bed. I planned the holiday so I could come home quickly with the dogs if it all went pear-shaped.

My fears were unfounded as both dogs were fantastically well behaved and I

could not have been more proud of them. 😍🤩 Nothing fazed Oberon, he just took everything in his stride with no struggles at all. So much so that when my daughter came home slightly before us, as planned, I made the decision to let Othello come back with her (emotionally a very tough decision). This gave me the opportunity to assess how much of Oberon's confidence came from Othello. Surprisingly, it appeared that not much of it came from him! If anything, he was even more chilled!

Anyway, to get to the point of my ramblings …

I have still been unable to walk Othello by himself, as Oberon would go into full blown howling and meltdown even when one of the children was with him (I should say young adults really 😂). Very occasionally, I've grabbed a few minutes with Othello, but I do mean very occasionally. When we came back from holiday I decided to try again with Oberon and erected the holiday crate in the sitting room and began placing his food bowl in there with delicious smelly tinned dog food. Yesterday, I popped him in the crate, covered it down and went for a walk with Othello, leaving my daughter sitting quietly in the room. He whined a tiny bit and did a howl at a dog barking outside. But other than that, he was quiet. 😁 Today, I repeated the process at a different time and the only noise he made was a sigh as he settled down. 🤩🤩🤩🤩 I am not naive enough to think it will always be like this, but I am elated. 😁😁

Lots of love,
Carrie xxx

30th July 2020

I've been using my best puppy dog eyes because Carrie is giving me a serious bear-stare!!

Carrie was just about to take me for a walk while Oberon was quiet in his crate, and guess what????
Terry turned up with his three dogs 🤣🤣

We were so excited to see one another that we went into full-on crazy.
It was bliss 😊
Every dog was barking, LD was howling in his crate and we got so overwhelmed that we chewed Carrie's honeysuckle off to nearly the ground.
I think she's a bit cross as she planted it 20 years ago ... oops 😐
I was actually very calm to begin with, but Terry was a bit upset that I wasn't super pleased to see him, so I let him perk me up.

I think Carrie is gnashing her teeth which personally I find impolite 😂😂

Yours, breathlessly,
Othello xxx

31st July 2020 Carrie into online dog training group

The Oberon Stretch Gauge

Chapter 2. 😂😂

"After the holiday!"
Running away feelings: Zero. Not even a fast skip into the sunset. 😁
Reduced to tears: Zero. 👍👍👍👍
Laughs: Countless! His newest pleasure is wood bark. So much fun can be found in throwing it around and pouncing on it. Training on wood bark is encouraging me to work on my frustration levels, because it is way more exciting than I am. 😉
Recall: 99% unless wood bark is involved. 😂
Kibble: Remember kibble? Well, it's definitely a thing of the past. Grain free tinned dog food has been the "in thing" for the last week with no signs of change. Makes training with food interesting. Still taking it as a huge win though. All considerations of replacing previous, Unicorn-riding, employee have been put firmly on the back burner. 😂
Mud: Glorious mud. So deeply beneficial in keeping his coat that much sought-after apricot colour. 😂

Resource guarding: Zero.
How many more puppies will I get: Accidentally clicked on an advert for fox red Labrador pups yesterday so I got a newspaper out and beat the idea out of my head … again. 😂😂
Howling incidents: Virtually none, I say that in a very "lower case" voice so as not to jinx it. 😂😂 Although unexpected "Terry Time" did provoke some. To be fair that wasn't only Oberon it was me too, at the loss of my beloved honeysuckle plant and the complete bedlam that ensued. One dog digging up my border, one dog chasing my cat, one dog jumping fences. I won't be naming dog names of course. My Terrible Terriers were elated to join in with the barking fest just to add another level of manic behaviour. 😂 After the visit I took myself to my boundary and chanted "Square Words" to calm myself down.
Wine to be consumed this weekend: Will entirely depend on whether we get anymore "Terry Time" this week. 😂😂

Lots of love,
Carrie xxx

Chapter Eleven
'A moose loose aboot the hoose'

1st August 2020

Morning!

I had a blast yesterday morning while LD stayed at home in his crate!
Whoop, whoop! Right?
I was so happy to have 1-2-1 with Carrie.
Even in the river I kept my eyes on her just in case she ran off or got lost (we know how good she is at that don't we? 😂😂😂)
It was super hot, so the river was the place to be 😁

Before the walk, I had a scatter feed outside and pretended it had spread far enough for me to tidy up after the cats.

Incidentally, they had left some entrails in the conservatory and although we didn't get Carrie's entrail dance (which is often a firm favourite of mine) we did get the reflex gag song 😂😂😂

Stay cool.

Lots of love,
Othello xxx

2nd August 2020

Oberon here.
Yesterday we went to Cardiff to dwop Jos stuff at her new house.
Went for a walk.
Saw dogs.
Not bark.
Saw lots of dwopped food in de street.
Not allowed to eat it 😱
Got HUMPED by a dog 😦
E did not even intwoduce imself first!!!

Wuv U

3rd August 2020

Morning from Othello.

It was an early start for us today as it's another one if those Please Don't Talk days.

LD and I had a walk when all the smells were nice and fresh in the forest.
We both had to try our very hardest not to track a hare after we got scent of it.
When it appeared and ran off up the trail, there was some serious consideration of our options 😊 so Carrie had to get her best crazy behaviour on and had some super fish treats ready for us 😂
Even after that we were still sniffing the air, so those treats had to keep coming our way 😁

We've been lying quietly for hours now with the occasional bout of alertness when something happens outside.

I'm not saying we're doing it on purpose, but it does result in nice treats if we look alert 😉
Some very tasty chews came our way too.
I gobbled mine down quickly and eyed up LD's, but I knew he would dob on me for stealing it!

We are off for a gallop around the field now, to get rid of the cobwebs 😍

Love and contented sighs,
Othello xxx

4th August 2020

Good morning from Othello.

LD came with us on the walk today which meant I had to set a good example.
Almost the first thing we saw were some sheep who were resting by MY river.
I say "were" because they got up and ran off when they saw us.
They are such silly, flutter brained creatures!

Apparently, me ignoring them and then sitting nicely is a big thing and worth lots of treats and fuss.
Personally, I don't get it as I've seen thousands of sheep before and I was just glad they weren't in my river, because sheep smell 🤪

After Carrie had cleared up the inevitable mouse entrails, we started this morning off with some leg weaves and you know how I feel about them 👎👎👎 but I played along for the laughs and the treats 😉
There are plenty of laughs, as Carrie tries to encourage me but not fall over 😊

Don't tell the others this, but when someone asked Carrie why she didn't just walk all us dogs together she said it was because her favourite time was just having time with me 😊

I am very responsible and always keep a close eye on her so I expect she feels safe 😁

Have a good day.

Yours, smugly,
Othello xxx

5th August 2020

Oberon here.
I ave been bathed.
I ave been airdryed.
I ave been snipped.
And bwushed.
I did fall asweep 😊
Thello sez I smellz.

6th August 2020

Light bulb moment!
After being very confused, I think I have finally got this agility stuff!
It's like ten pin bowling where I act as the ball 😂😂
I'm getting much better at knocking the weave poles over, but I haven't got them all yet.
It's fabulous fun, Carrie ambles around like a hippo while waving a treat!
I follow close behind totally focused on where the hippo is going.
Well, to be honest I'm all eyes on the treat but no need to mention that to Carrie.

She likes to think I'm transfixed by her elegant moves 

Yours, happily,
Othello xxx

7th August 2020

The Oberon Stretch Gauge

Week 12

Running away feelings: Zero.
Reduced to tears: Zero.
Laughs: Countless. Yesterday evening we went for a walk in my childhood woods and he did a wonderful impression of a gazelle as he pronked through the undergrowth. Sheer joy and gay abandon in every jump.
Recall: 99% We are currently away for a few days in unfamiliar surroundings, so yesterday's pronking did make him go deaf for a few seconds.
Kibble: This old chestnut again!!! Still loving the tinned food but has to have previously "disgusted at" kibble sprinkled on top. It has to be rotated anti clockwise twice, clockwise once (on previously mentioned silver salver) and dropped from height of approximately five centimetres (see how flexible he is becoming).
Mud: He is not allowed near any until a full two days have gone by, post grooming.
Resource guarding: Zero.
How many more puppies will I get: Fox red labs are gorgeous.
Howling incidents: A couple of nano howls when left in his crate so I could walk Othello, but he settled himself.
Wine: Well, I am on a mini break.
Oberon is proving himself to be super-flexible and more optimistic about life by the day.
We're in England at the moment and he has not been at all fazed by people in

masks, staying in a hotel or walking in new locations (early days though as we only arrived yesterday evening 🙈).

Lots of love,
Carrie xxx

8th August 2020 Carrie into the online dog training group

Sometimes we miss a win, but today I'm celebrating taking a shower without LD making any fuss. Yes, he was in the bathroom but we're at an hotel and he couldn't see me because of the shower curtain. A new environment, and me being even slightly separated from him, would previously have been a crisis for him. He's done this twice now, so I'm really proud of him.
That might not seem like much but a few months ago he would have been in meltdown mode!

Lots of love,
Carrie xxx

Morning!
Since we got here I ave been to de woods lots.
And to de canal.
And to some standing stones witch r good for peeing on.
I fink whoever put dem der wiked dogs😄😄

Wuv U

9th August 2020 Carrie into online dog training group

This post is not meant in any way to sound smug, it's meant purely to give anyone who is struggling hope.
I think it's really important for anyone who has a challenging dog to know that YOU, YES YOU, are not alone and that things really can change for the better.

Oberon has been one of the greatest challenges I have ever faced in my life. Almost a greater challenge than supporting my dearest friend through her battle against cancer. He is my 13th dog and the one that nearly broke my confidence as a dog owner. I consider myself to be a pretty strong person; I've raised my three children alone for five days a week as my husband has only ever been at home at weekends (until lockdown). The oldest is now 22, and I also have two teenage boys, so I'm no stranger to challenges. 😂

Since I got Oberon (aka LD) in December, he has reduced me to tears more than once. I can be honest and say that there have been occasions when I haven't been that fond of him 😂, and also felt that getting him was a huge mistake. For months, my thoughts were jangling through lack of sleep (because I was worrying so much about his struggles) and I was exhausted from trying different ways to help him cope and also balance the needs of the rest of my pack (and family). There have been times when putting him into boarding kennels for a few days to get a break has been a tempting thought, but my heart has kept telling me that neither of us would feel better for that. Don't get me wrong, I do believe that we need to "put our own oxygen masks on first", and that sometimes a break might be the best thing, but I've not actually quite got there yet. I've reprimanded myself for thinking with my heart instead of my head and not examining the impact of taking what I knew was a troubled puppy. I felt like any possible struggle a dog could have, from permanent diarrhoea to Separation Anxiety, from fear of the outside world to resource guarding, were all thrown at Oberon.

Through ever struggle though there has been this little soul who has loved me with all his tiny heart. He has always just wanted a cuddle and a hug. He finds his comfort and reassurance in me, and that is a great honour to have bestowed on me. His enthusiasm for life is second to no other dog I have ever

met. He loves playing games, learns easily, and is more than willing to show his new skills off. 😂😂He is the complete opposite of Othello, who really drags his feet sometimes until he sees the treats. 😂😂 Oberon will play just for the sheer love of playing.

Oberon now embraces (nearly) everything new with the enthusiasm of a pessimist turned optimist. Pub gardens: No worries. Other dogs: No worries. Holidays: No worries. New walks: No worries. New people: No worries. 😁 Every single one a win that I could never have imagined in my wildest dreams. 💕💕

When I joined this group last August, I saw posts from people who had turned their challenging dogs around, but I always thought there must be something special about them. I assumed they must have some deep, as-yet-untapped intuition that they had simply now found to guide them on their journey. It had to be some hidden talent that they possessed, or they were just better than me. But with the help of Tom (his amazing consult, and his wonderful optimism), Lauren (her constant enthusiasm), and this group, I've helped to make my dogs lives better – and mine too. There must also be a mention for Rupert's mum. We have shared many laughs and moans about our challenging boys. 😘😘

So, if you feel like you're losing, remember anyone can change their dog's life. Stay strong and trust the process. It will happen. 💕💕

I envisage many more challenges to come, as Oberon is reaching adolescence, so I will try to keep reminding myself how far we have already come. 😁😁

Lots of love,
Carrie xxx

10th August 2020

Oberon here.
I wantz a King size bed wike de hotel one wen I getz home

I also wantz a canal.
An a standin stone.
Sum weally big fishy treats.
An a pony.

Wuv U

11th August 2020

Hello from a very hot Wales.

I was super pleased to see Carrie when she picked me up from the kennels yesterday.
I visited Auntie Joan for a few days, because I would not have enjoyed going to the hotel.
I think LD was a bit disappointed about coming home as he enjoyed being an only dog.
He's got to share Carrie with me and the other guys again now, so I envisage a sulk 😉

I was a bit put out earlier myself.
I was lying on my raised bed in the shade and silly Carrie tipped water on it.
She said it was to cool me down, but I jumped off and refused to get back on it!
Why on earth would I want to lie in water?
She clearly does not understand that water games are meant for rivers, pools or puddles.

I'm joining in with LD's sulk now!

Love from, a slightly disgruntled,

Othello xxx

12th August 2020

Good morning!

Carrie and I were up with the larks this morning and went for a lovely walk.
I did some sniffing of trails and searching for treats.
It was cool enough for some ball fetching too 😁

There were places where I had to go into stealth mode, because Carrie was hoping to see deer, but they must have all gone back to bed.

We had one minor misunderstanding when I thought Carrie told me to go and swim in the muddy pool, but it turns out that's not what she said 😂😂

Lots of love,
Othello xxx

13th August 2020

Ad a walk wiv just Cawwie.
Dog ran up and barked at I.
I did not bark.
Cawwie went out wiv Thello.
I did owl😒

Wuv U

14th August 2020 Carrie into online dog training group

The Oberon Stretch Gauge

Week 13

Running away feelings: 0 to 0.25 …
Reduced to tears: Zero.
Laughs: Countless, but probably the funniest was when he found a frog after a storm. There followed a few minutes of curiosity followed by leaping back a few inches, while I tried to activate my phone's torch (Why is it so impossible to locate the torch icon?). He was fascinated by this little bouncy creature but not entirely convinced that its motives were innocent. Evidence of some optimism on his part 😁 however, I suspect the frog will become a pessimist forever.😭
Recall: 99% Definitely hitting "adolescent boy" phase though; peeing on anything and everything outside requires absolute focus! The three legged "Dance to the Hormone God" is a frequent occurrence ... sniff, stick nose in further, raise leg, circle some more, add a nose twitch and release. 😂 "Was Cawwie sayin summink?"
Kibble: Othello's kibble is suitable for training purposes. Tinned food is devoured and then any remnants left in his beard lovingly wiped around the back of my bare legs. 😱
Mud: The storms have brought mud a-plenty, but the hot weather has called for river swimming, so problem resolved to everyone's satisfaction. 😁
Resource guarding: This is back to rear its ugly head this week. An incident with a stolen sock which Oberon and Othello were playing tug with resulted in a growl. Teenage son, being "the keeper of all knowledge", felt his approach to retrieving said sock by the "shout and grab method" was preferable to any "girly, hair ribbon twisting" advice I could offer. 😕 Not a method I would ever recommend. Extra vigilance required. 😭
How many more puppies will I get? I've heard that stick insects make good pets. 👍👍
Howling incidents: A few when left in his crate so I could walk Othello. On the plus side, he scarfs down his cheese biscuits before howling … progress,

as eating under stress has been a no-no before (gotta try and find a win in there somewhere 😂😂)
Wine: Who am I trying to kid? I'm going to pour it into a punch bowl and chuck in a few mint leaves. 😂😂

Happy weekend. 😘

Lots of love,
Carrie xxx

15th August 2020

Good morning from a slightly wet Othello.

It was early walking for us this morning and a tiny moment when we forgot our manners and went to chase a hare … oops 😔
We came straight back and gobbled down some treats.

Anyway, now we're home I'm taking up observation duty.
I am staring at the point I first saw "the mouse".
I was sitting on the sofa the day before yesterday, when I saw the mouse chilling under the woodburner.
We've been telling Carrie about it for a few days, but she thought we were watching a spider.
It's been living inside the sofa in a very sweet little nest, so we thought Carrie must have put it there.
She's always taking in little lost animals!
I think it's been eating our kibble that's rolled under there, but we are more than happy to share with a soul in need.
I'm not going to make any observation about Carrie's housekeeping skills here 😉
I think the cats must have brought it in because it had a little cut on its tail.
It must have needed to recuperate somewhere safe with a nice supply of yummy food.

As you know, I'm a big fan of most little animals so I really wanted us to be friends 😁
Apparently though, mice should not roam freely indoors. I know it's crazy isn't it? 🤔
There was much excitement as Carrie, Jo, and the teenage boys, pursued it around the room.
It finally went back into its nest where they caught it, after they'd done some alterations to the bottom of the sofa 😉
As there is a much bigger hole for it to live in now I'm hoping that it comes back with some friends 🤞😁

Have a lovely day.

Yours, vigilantly,
Othello xxx

16th August 2020

Oberon here
I Ignored Cawwie coz I waz chasing a bird and I wiked it 😆😆
She sez I iz a tewwible teen an she az enuff of dem already 😉

Wuv U

17th August 2020

Fortunately, we had our walk early before the rain came.

LD had to stay on the lead because he has found that birds are interesting to chase.
He's a bit of a fool. I conserve energy and stay close for free treats 😂

I've also had treats for staying on my bed while Carrie was playing games with LD ... there is an energy saving theme here that I really love 😁

No sign of the mouse returning yet 😔 but I'm staying hopeful 😀
I thought it was back last night as LD was watching something in the corner but, much to Carrie's distress, it was a huge spider that disappeared under the sofa 😂😂😂
I anticipate much excitement tonight when it comes back out 🤣

Lots of love,
Othello xxx

18th August 2020

Good morning from Othello

The day has only just started, but I'm exhausted from joining in with Carrie's workout.
I'm all for easing myself into the day but that's not how we roll here.
It's up and at 'em, with no chance of returning for a snooze.

Had a very wet walk yesterday evening, we all got soaking wet and were glad to get home.
The rain was hammering it down and we were feeling very sorry for ourselves.
To be honest, a swim in the river would have been much more fun.

No sign of my mouse or the spider yesterday evening 😔
I reckon the spider has moved into Carrie's bedroom, but don't tell her 🤣😂

Slobbery kisses,
Othello xxx

19th August 2020

Morning!

After much consideration (actually not that much, I was just trying to sound thoughtful 😂), I've concluded that LD is just a goodie-two-shoes.

We've been having a game-playing session.
As you know, I spend a lot of time trying to act foolish (or "a bit twp" as we say around here), as I have found that I can get a lot of treats that way 😉
Now, LD just loves to get it right, and frankly he's showing me up and I'm not that happy about it.

Take the training button for instance.

Carrie wants us to push it, so I glance at it sometimes and get a treat.
Mostly, I've got my attention on Carrie's treat hand though 😂😂
Makes sense doesn't it? That's where all the goodies come from 😁
She is very happy with my "pretend" interest and I get rewarded handsomely, so we're both happy.

However, LD is ringing that bell like a pro.
I reckon he thinks he's royalty and Carrie is his woman servant.

He rings it with such enthusiasm, it's like he actually enjoys it 😱
I'm going to have a quiet word with him later and tell him his fortune, and it's not looking good for him at the moment.
I predict a mud accident coming along shortly after his next visit to the groomer 🤣 shhh

Love from, your long suffering friend,
Othello xxx

20th August 2020

We iz going to kennels today and haz to stay overnight.
I iz not sure I will wike dat, but Thello sez itz OK.
I iz not sure if I should bark and owl a lot.
Yesterday I did bark at a dog wen it appeared from nowhere.
I dont fink I should ave dun dat.
I did not owl in mys cwate wen Cawwie walked Thello.
I iz a gud boy 😊

Wuv U

20th August 2020

I did "turn taking" with Truffles this morning.
Turn taking is a bit difficult for me because it is my frisbee!

Truffles had something called "a stroke" earlier on in the month and was a bit unwell.
She's feeling like playing again now, but we have to make it short sessions.
Apart from holding her head a bit to one side, and being a bit wobbly sometimes, she is very happy😁

Truffles is a great big sister and taught me a lot about manners when I was a pup!
Let's just say that puppies are not her favourite creatures and you learn to behave quickly 😉

Lots of love,
Othello xxx

21st August 2020

The Oberon Stretch Gauge

Week 14

Running away feelings: Zero.
Reduced to tears: Zero.
Laughs: Countless, with garden plant pots being a great source of delight, especially if filled with one of my favourite plants. 😱
Recall: Having lived surrounded by birds for the last 8 months, Oberon has finally tuned into them, and they are full-blown chasing fun … recall is brilliant if we are inside the house, unless there is a spider around … or a fly. 😂😂😂 DMT back in play big-time at home. Lots of crazy games outside to get that focus back.
Kibble: He loves it, if sprinkled delicately on top of his tinned food as a garnish (we've been here before!) and best of all if it's from Othello's food bag. 😉
Mud: Not too bad this week, but Othello has predicted (after some sibling rivalry) that there would be at least one incident post Oberon's visit to the groomer next week. 😂😂😂
Resource guarding: Zero! He's redeemed himself after last week's sock theft and has been an angel. 😊
Puppies: There are some very nice collies at my sister-in-law's farm. They're renowned for being super laid back. Aren't they? 😂😂😂
Howling: Zero.
Wine: It's the weekend again. 😉😉
A pretty good week!
Oberon and Othello were in kennels last night and I'm collecting them later so fingers crossed!

All was well at 2200 last night, and Auntie Joan said that she would tell them that mummy called to say goodnight.

Lots of love,
Carrie xxx

22nd August 2020 Carrie into the online dog training group

What can I say?

Mine have to be the cutest dogs out there. 

I know it's been said by many people and many times before, but if you want to feel true love you need a dog (or five) in your life.

When I picked my boys up from kennels yesterday evening, I was almost drowned in furry cuddles and kisses. Oberon could not have cuddled closer unless we morphed into one person, and Othello's whole body was wagging with delight. The overnight stay was a success.

It's taken me months to build up the courage to leave Oberon overnight. He had a taster day last week where he was there from late morning to early evening, but overnight felt like a huge step. Othello is an old paw at it so I wasn't concerned about him, but I was worried that Oberon would be broken by it. They shared a pen and I took a divider, so they could be close without Othello feeling pestered. They both had blankets which had my scent on.

Oberon is certainly more clingy at the moment but that's understandable, we will just do some chilling for a few days.

They're having another overnighter next week and I will gradually build the days up until I can have a long weekend away without being a gibbering wreck.

Super proud of Othello for being such a calming influence on Oberon and super proud of Oberon for coping so well.

Lots of love,
Carrie xxx

23rd August 2020

Since our trip to kennels I have been enjoying my home comforts 😁
I'm hoping Carrie starts to realise that I need a sofa if I go to kennels again 😂

I decided to toughen up on LD while we were away and when I found a rawhide chew in the outside run, I refused to give it to him and held on tight.
I gave it to Auntie Joan when she asked though.
We don't have rawhide chews at home, so I was happy to find it 😏

I was hoping my pet mouse would return while we were away but still no sign ☹
There was a huge spider under Carrie's pillow last night though 😂
I was super impressed at the speed she moved even with her extra lockdown inertia 🤣
I wasn't allowed to keep the spider as a pet 😢

We've been relaxing at home, so I don't have much to report.
Yesterday evening we went to the field. LD was super barky and was racing around after smells.
Have a great day,

Love,
Othello xxx

24th August 2020

Me an Thello az been aving to sit quietly on our waised beds while Cawwie waz studying again 😔
I did bark at de man who came to do fencing, but I did not bark at some dogs I saw dis morning 😋 I fink dat balanced it out 😆

Wuv U 

25th August 2020

Morning!

An early walk in the rain for Carrie and me while LD was still asleep.

I'm really starting to feel that the work I've put in with Carrie is paying off!!
About time if you ask me 🤣
We were playing a few games and Carrie was reloading her hand with treats.
She missed what she thinks was a little critter running across the road.
Not me though, I spotted it and gave chase only to hear the word that sings like an angel in my ear "ball".
I stopped like I'd seen a bear in the bush and turned tail and ran back to be rewarded with a fantastic ball game.
You know how much I love a ball 😁

Of course, only I know if there actually was a critter or if I was just rehearsing a bit of behaviour I would like from Carrie 😉
Happy days.

Snuffles,
Othello xxx

26th August 2020

I went to de gwoomerz yesterday an I got wewy tired.
It misses Cawwie wen she iznt wiv i.
I needed lots of hugs an cuddles wen I got home.

Cawwie has been telling de Boy for agez not to leave is book on de sofa coz I might eat it.

I wikes paper wewy mutch 😁
I ate de cover, just to prove Cawwie right u understand 🤣😄
I iz wewy elpful 😁

Wuv U

26th August 2020

Wen Cawwie walked in I waz sitting on mys bed nicely and Thello waz wriggling on de sofa.
I iz a wewy good boy 😄😄😄

Wuv U

27th August 2020

We played at agility this morning, but my heart wasn't completely in it.

There was a lovely smell in the air, and it was very distracting.
I think it might be something the cats despatched.
I tried to find that smell yesterday, but Carrie spotted me.
Worry not though, I will track it down.
I feel like it's going to be worth a quick snaffle and a shoulder-dipping roll.
I have plans to introduce LD and his perfectly coiffured coat to it as well.
If you remember I promised an outcome for him being such a goodie-two-shoes 😉😂
Shhhhh though 😜

Your friend,
Othello xxx

28th August 2020 Carrie into online dog training group

The Oberon stretch gauge

Week 15

Running away feelings: Zero.
Reduced to tears: Zero.
Laughs: Countless, as fun is LD's main agenda, and he can find it anywhere. A leaf blowing in the wind is as exciting as a new best friend. 💕 Everything he does starts with a spin and a bounce, he anticipates joy around every corner. A far cry from the little man who was scared of literally everything. 💕
Recall: Well, he is definitely in the throws of adolescent independence. Yes, he comes back – but at his leisure after he's " just been over there" because there was a very exciting smell. Management is key 😂 so I spend a lot of time hiding behind trees like a sad dog stalker. He might be independent, but only if he knows exactly where I am. 😂😂 I walk around with the smell of decomposing body parts wafting into the air around me as only the most disgusting smelling treats will cut the mustard. On the plus side, people will be reluctant to stop to chat to us so we will get longer walks. 😂
Kibble: I'm able to mix it into his tinned food this week and it's being eaten with gusto😁 (Gusto being his appetite rather than some random critter that lives under the sofa 😉).
Mud: Avoided at all costs as he came back from the groomer looking too cute for words. Othello still has plans to change this asap having scouted out a dead animal smell. 😱
Resource guarding: Zero.
Puppies: Life is becoming calmer, so I think I won't rock the boat. 😉
Howling: Zero. I suspect this is because I haven't put him in a situation where he needed to though, as I wanted to keep him calm prior to visiting the groomer. Same again before his second overnighter at the kennels (last night).

**Update from Kennels … "Good as gold, bless them". 😁😁😁😁
Wine: Yes please, thank you very much.👍💕
Happy weekend. 💕

Lots of love,
Carrie xxx

<u>29th August 2020</u>

Afternoon!

We got home late last night after our trip away to the kennels.

Carrie and I thought the mouse was back because LD was super excited and all of a wag about something behind his bed, it turned out to be a spider the size of a terrier though 😂😂😂
I had to laugh at the fuss Carrie made. She nearly spilled her wine 😂😂
Before Carrie plucked up the courage to catch it, the spider got broken by LD when he got over friendly with it. He then spent ages trying to get it to go again 😐

We're having a chill day today as everyone is a bit tired.

Lots of love,
Othello xxx

<u>30th August 2020</u>

I'm disappointed in LD's behaviour.

Since we've come back from kennels, he's been rather vocal.
We saw another dog when we were walking this morning.
Of course, I just went to Carrie's side when she called.

However, LD (who was on the lead for a previous barking misdemeanour) barked at it!!

He then jumped out of the car when we got home without being given the cue. Course he had to get back in then, and this was eating into my nap time.

On the plus side, he is making me look very good 😉

Yours, smugly,
Othello xxx

<u>31st August 2020</u>

A nice early start for us today, while LD was still sleeping.
We played loads of ball and then some no-rules fun.
Carrie was scattering food around with gay abandon and I was hoovering it up like a pro.

More "Please Don't Talk" going on now 😂😂😂

Lots of love,
Othello xxx

Autumn
22nd Sept – 21st Dec
2020

Chapter Twelve
'Rainbows and Celebrations'

1st September 2020

Morning!

More early morning fun while LD was sleeping.
We played a game where I had to wait in Middle then Carrie threw the ball and I had to be patient until she gave the release cue.
I've played this game loads before, but I still prefer just rushing off after the ball!
After I've raced after the ball and brought it back, I'm supposed to put it into Carrie's hand.
However, I've heard that bending down to pick it up will help get rid of some of her lockdown inertia.
In the interest of improving her health, I just drop it and act dumb.
Why keep a Carrie and pick up the ball yourself?

Yours, lovingly,
Othello xxx

I iz on high alert for a new spyder.
I miss de bwoken one.
In fact I iz on high alert for anyfink.
Thello says I iz behavin wike a twonk.
I fink e eard Cawwie say dat to mys fwiend Wupert's Mum.

Wuv U

2nd September 2020

Morning!

I've been doing an early workout with Carrie.
I have to say after YEARS of working out, she still can't get her foot behind her ear like I can.
I have zero idea why she still keeps waving her legs in the air and saying that stretching is good!
I put my fitness down to all the hours I've invested in scrabbling onto and under things to find any morsel of food.
I sense a diet coming on and I hate that when her clothes are tighter, I have to go on a diet too!

Your friend,
Othello xxx

3rd September 2020

I have been out for a walk with my big sister Truffles this morning.

When I was a puppy she taught me a lot about manners because she really does not like puppies in her space.
She's my best friend now!
Not my bestest friend, of course, because that's Terry 

We were both poised with excitement this morning!
Carrie kept running off in different directions in the forest.
I think she imagined she was like a graceful wood nymph.
In reality, she looked more like a demented purple leprechaun!

At one point Carrie was super-focused on Truffles, which gave me an opportunity to explore.
I went on a mission to scout out a very nice smell at the bottom of a tree.
I soon realised that its fragrance was "Eau de decomposing critter".
I was just about to do a shoulder-dip when Carrie called me back.
I have marked its precise location, so I'll reap its benefits next time.

We left LD at home because his "special little personality" gets a bit much for Truffles sometimes 😊
I understand that while we were away, he entertained everyone with his favourite song ☹

Lots of love,
Othello xxx

4th September 2020

The Oberon stretch gauge

Week 16

Running away feeling: 0 to 0.25
Reduced to tears: Zero.
Laughs: Countless. We're still just about winning with more laughs than under-breath-muttering, but it's been a tough week. ☹ 😊 😊

Recall: I'm still in sad stalker mode and he's still in his Alexa mode of "Sorry I don't understand that". Of course, he always returns but with the swagger of a teenager who's only doing it because he actually wants to, not because his mum asked him to. 😉
Kibble: "Nope, not going to touch that, it's probably been doped by a dog catcher".
Mud: Ha! One up for me! He's still clean after his trip to the groomer last week. Much puddle management has taken place. 😉
Puppies: Nope, nope, nope! Stick insects are back in the running.
Howling: What can I say? This week has definitely been a punishing one after my night away last week.
He's been super vigilant about everything. Permanently on the alert; not barking, fortunately, but clearly ready to do so. I left it for four days before I risked leaving him in his crate to have some time with Othello in actual daylight, rather than early morning with night vision goggles. 😊
I encouraged him into his crate with endearing words, super delicious treats, and tucked the blanket around the crate. I even put calming music on (but stopped myself from lighting scented candles and producing an 8°C Chablis). I walked off into the daylight with my trusty Labrador by my side, feeling like someone about to conquer a new world. I could almost hear the fanfair playing …(Yes, I did walk fast until I was out of hearing distance). I returned feeling like a Viking warrior, only to find that my home-coming fanfair was less joyous and was actually more of a grunt. The teenagers reported in their unique language that the darling puppy "Ad bin owlin, right"
Wine: Would dearly love some but after all Othello's hints I've decide that I had better shed the lockdown weight. If you listen carefully you will no doubt hear me gnawing at the skirting boards later.

So, in the interest of camaraderie it's over to you guys to do it for me.
Cheers!

Lots of love,
Carrie xxx

5th September 2020

I ave been playing games in de garden dis mornin, wiv frisbees.
I wuved to cat a bit too mutch an it stuck itz scwatchy fings in I.
Next time I will old it down better (dont tell Cawwie I sed dat😉).

Wuv U

6th September 2020

Carrie took a photo of me with a rainbow and said that I am the pot of gold at the end of it!

We went for a walk, just the two of us, in the forest!
I coerced her into just playing ball by gazing up at her and then sticking my nose into her pocket.
She finally got the idea, and we had a blast.
In gratitude for her compliance, I resisted rolling in cow poo 😊

It's fair to say that she is picking up my training hints more quickly these days 😊

Lots of love,
Othello xxx

7th September 2020

Good morning!

We were up with the larks again today to get in extra training before LD woke up.
When he gets up, the crazy begins.

Getting 1-2-1 with Carrie is still difficult when he's awake, 'cos he sticks to her like a slug to a window.

We played the game where she dashes off and hides if I'm not watching her.
While she was fumbling with the treats a man with a dog came around the corner.
I didn't break off staring at her hand even when she stopped to chat with him.
Luckily, I was able to disengage her by drooling and whining a bit while displaying my best puppy dog eyes 😊

Doggy snuffles,
Othello xxx

8th September 2020

I az been a bit poorly wiv sickness and flat poos.
I fink itz coz I eated sumfing yummy from de ground yesterday.
I getz lots of cuddles though so I dont mind.

9th September 2020

Fank u for your wuverly get well messegez.
I feel mutch better today.
I az ad chickin dis morning an I did not womit.
I iz wewy appy coz I wuv chickin.
I did chase a bird in de woodz but went back wen Cawwie called I.
I did chase it again 😊

Wuv U 

10th September 2020:

I had a frisbee session with Truffles this morning.

Because I was feeling generous, I even let her carry it.
I'm positively angelic sometimes 😉
She is super speedy at getting to the frisbee first, but usually I just push her out of the way and run back with it.

I am thinking of faking a tummy ache later so I can get some of LD's chicken.
If that doesn't work, I'll knock the lid off the cat biscuit tin and tidy them up.

Shhhh.

Hugs,
Othello xxx

11th September 2020

The Oberon Stretch Gauge

Week 17

Running away feelings: Zero.
Reduced to tears: Zero.
Laughs: Countless. He tested chilli powder in a very optimistic way, had a serious sneezing fit and a very nasty taste in his mouth. He got told off by Othello for being in his face too much, so he came and tucked his head under my arm in an attempt to become an Ostrich.
Recall: For the first minute of being off the lead he is dead to anything I say while he runs back and forth like a toddler on coffee shots. After that he hangs off my every word as long as there are no feathery things around, in which case I have to pull out all the stops, make myself super interesting and rain sprats from the sky at the same time.
Kibble: He's sticking to his dog catcher theory.
Mud: Only made it as high as the top of his legs. He discovered what could easily have been a hippo's hollow.
Puppies: Nope, just Nope!
Howling: His day crate is currently the equivalent of a maximum-security prison to him. No amount of delicious treats will convince him to step in there, let alone eat in there. Not eating is a sign that we have taken a step back, so I need to work on upping the crate's value again.
Wine: Still on the lard-arse reduction diet so not a drop will pass my lips. On the bright side I will have saved enough money to replace the skirting boards that I gnawed before.
He and Othello did behave like angels while a man was fitting a new floor. He was asked to ignore them and he did, so they ignored him too.

Lots of love,
Carrie xxx

12th September 2020

Cawwie bought I a new tug toy.
I gwabbed it from her and and ran off wiv it.
She wanted I to swap it for anuvver tug but I didn't.
I wiked dat game and played it for agez.
Cawwie did sum mutterwing.

Wuv U

13th September 2020

Afternoon!

**I had a very nice game of frisbee with Carrie.
She was chasing after the frisbee too but isn't as fast as me.
I had to do a bit of impulse-control and wait to be told to fetch it.
That's OK though, I can be very patient if it's worth it 😉**

**Today was duck cleaning-out day, so I had a fantastic rummage around on the muck heap until Carrie spotted me.
I won't disclose how much tidying up I managed before she saw me though 😉**

**Your friend,
Othello xxx**

14th September 2020

I iz a good boy.

We met a lady wiv sum dogs an dey gwowled at I but I just ignored dem.
Den I got barked at by annuver dog.
He iz always cwoss an barks at I.
I just ignored im too.
See ow good I iz?

Wuv U

15th September 2020

Truffles and I had to work hard on self-control today.
Firstly, we walked down a track after a cow had been leaving presents on it.
Then we didn't even chase an otter that we saw disappearing into a ditch.
I'll let you make up your own minds about whether the liver treats Carrie had with her influenced our choices 😉
Whatever our motives were didn't really matter; as Carrie was super impressed with us.
We're both very wise and know that storing up some points is always worthwhile.
We can have the odd indiscretion later without Carrie being bothered.
With this knowledge firmly in the front of our minds, we felt justified in snaffling up the bag of treats that she left unattended.

Lots of love,
Othello xxx

16th September 2020

LD and I were woken up at "sparrow fart" to drive to Cardiff.

We went to pick up Jo as she's coming home for the weekend.
The early morning was worth it as she shares her house and garden with other students.
"Why would that make it worth it?" I hear you ask yourselves.
Well, students can be carefree when it comes to leaving food scattered around.
They can also be carefree about emptying their bins 😉
It was positively dog heaven and both LD and I found some super tasty delights.
LD found something called "dog ends" in the street but they turned out to be very nasty tasting.
I'm glad he tasted them first.

Slobbery kisses,
Othello xxx

17th September 2020

Good morning from Othello

Agility first thing! What a joke!
I had to jump poles, weave in and out, and walk on a ladder.
Then I had to spin around and dive into the tunnel.

Carrie muttered something about the weave poles needing to be further apart.
She said someone was too fat to fit through them!

I politely resisted the temptation to point my paw at her 😉

Carrie wanted me to walk up and down the see-saw, but I declined.
It seems too much in the extreme sport vein for me!

Your friend,
Othello xxx

18th September 2020

The Oberon stretch gauge

Week 18

Running away feelings: Zero.
Reduced to tears: Why would I need to cry in exasperation? I have a cockapoo and he is so chilled. 😊
Laughs: Countless. The once fearful puppy is now as brave as a lion and has his nose into everything.
This week he helped the man with the plastering "If u ignore I den I will ave to get weally close to u". He sampled dog ends in the street. He is even responsible enough to have his own pet spider that visits every evening. We won't mention him jumping in the air because a piece of litter blew across the road.
Recall: "Ha!" Is what I say, I fly in the face of birds. I have a Tug-E-Nuff squeaky toy, and I am not afraid to use it. I walk around with it in my pocket like Wyatt Earp at the OK Coral. Go on birds, make my day, do your sexy, flirty, sassy fluttering and see what I draw from my holster.
Kibble: Oh yes!! Kibble is our friend. The kind of friend that you have just to play with. Eating it is just not a possibility.
Mud: He looks like a two-tone Cortina most days.
Resource Guarding: Zero. 😊
Puppies: I might move on to Shetland Ponies as they have such lovely natures. 😉
Howling: A tiny bit, but yesterday he stayed quietly on his raised bed while I took Othello to play in the garden for five minutes.
Wine: Party time tomorrow to celebrate my son's 18th Birthday and my successful completion of PDT. I am now officially a qualified Pro Dog Trainer!!!!

****

And thus draws the end of a year in our lives. I honestly never dreamed that 2020 would bring so much joy into my life or that I would achieve so much

to be proud of. There have been many tears shed, but they have been far outweighed by the laughs. However, I would never like to under-estimate how difficult our challenging dogs can be. Sometimes we have to dig really deep to find the much-needed humour that keeps us forging forward.

As I was working through the final edit prior to publication, I realised how very much further our journey has come since September. Othello is even more relaxed with life and Oberon's biggest struggles are 95% resolved (although kibble is still an ongoing battle 😉). Oberon's resource guarding is a thing of the past and his separation anxiety is vastly improved. We've all had more fun and games and our bond is even stronger.
Maybe that's all for another book …

I hope this book has brought a few smiles to your face. I also hope that I can go on and spread even more of what I've learned to any dog owners who are struggling. My career as a dog trainer is bringing me so much pleasure and the great reward of seeing dogs happier and enjoying much better lives.

With Much Love,
From
Carrie, Othello, Oberon, The Terrible Terriers and Truffles

He arrived and both our hearts were fragile
I sometimes had to fake a smile
I'd lost a friend and my heart was sore
But he needed me to hold his paw

Some days felt like they'd never end
He'd make me cry, he'd never bend
If I took a little step away
He'd whine and bark to make me stay

Some days he wouldn't let me rest
And he'd put my patience to the test
He'd take my stuff and then he'd growl
If I left for a second he'd cry, and howl

But every single stroke and restful cuddle
Brought us closer and healed the struggle
For every game and laugh we shared
We realised just how much we cared

And every moment we spend together
Makes HIM realise this IS forever
I'll not leave him and break his heart
But sometimes, we HAVE to part

He's surely not easy some of the time
But now it's a hill, not a mountain to climb
No one said love was the easiest choice
But I'll fight his corner, I'll be his voice

His trust, his grit, and his endless cheer
His love, his heart, his tiny fears
His optimism that's grown each day
His crazy, noisy, bouncy ways

They're all the things that brought us here
To the end of our first tumultuous year
I'm so very thankful to whoever decreed
That you get the dog you really need.

Oberon's Dictionary
Ad=Had
Airdryer=Hairdryer
Alwayz=Always
An=And

And=Hand
Annuver=Another
Appawently=Apparently
Appened=Happened
Appy=Happy
Ard = Hard
Arent=Aren't
Ave=Have
Az=As
Behavin=Behaving
Bendz=Bends
Bwuvver=Brother
Cant=Can't
Chickin=Chicken
Cide=Decide
Coz=Cos

Cwate=Crate
Cwoss=Cross
Cweeping=Creeping
Cwy=Cry
Dan=Than
Dat=That
De=The
Dem=Them
Der=There
Derservz=Deserves

Dey=They
Doeznt=Doesn't
Diculous=Ridiculous
Didnt=Didn't
Diffrent=Different
Dis=This
Doeznt=Doesn't
Dont=Don't
Dun=Done
Dwopped=Dropped
Ear=Hear
Eard=Heard
Eated=Ate
Enuff=Enough
Everybodys=Everybody
Everyfing=Everything
Fings=Things
Fink=Think
Fort=Thought
Frew=Threw
Fwiend=Friend
Getz=Get
Gwabbed=Grabbed
Gweat=Great
Gwow=Grow
Gwowled=Growled
Gwumpy=Grumpy

HaZ=Has
Im=Him
Imself=Himself
IndoorZ=Indoors
Intwoduce=Introduce
Iself/Myself
ItZ=Its/it's
IZ=Is
MessegeZ=Messages
Mite=Might
Mutch=Much
Mutterwing=Muttering
Mys=My

NeedZ=Needs
NoiseZ=Noises
Nuffin=Nothing
Old=Hold
Oped=Hoped
Ow=How
Owl=Howl
Owls=Howls
Preciate=Appreciate
Scwatchy=Scratchy
Sed=Said
Sez=Says
SmellZ=Smells

Spected=Expected
Spossed=Supposed
Sum=Some
Sumfing=something
Tending=Intending
Ticularly=Particularly
Til=Until
Twouble=Trouble
U=You
Undertsandz=Understands
Unger=Hunger
Uvver=Other
Waining=Raining
Waised=Raised
Wantsz=Wants
Waz=Was
Weach=Reach
Weally=Really
Weckon=Reckon
Wen=When
Wewy=Very
Wickle=Little
Wike=Like
Winstance= Instance
Witch=Which
Wiv=With
Wivout=Without

Woodz=Woods
Womit=Vomit
Wot=What
Wuverly=Lovely
Wud=Would
Wug=Rug
Wumbling=Rumbling
Wuv=Love
Wuverly=Lovely
Xcited=Excited
Xciting=Exciting

Printed in Great Britain
by Amazon